HANDS OFF

BY ATHENA HACKER

Cover design by Athena Hacker
Cover image contains AI imagery by Magic Media via Canva

Disclaimer: This book is not intended to act as a diagnosis, treatment, or definition of what touch-starvation is like.

Touch-starvation is a real issue that affects many across the world, particularly in the post-pandemic state of society.

This is simply a fictional story based on what one person's experience of loneliness and touch-starvation was like.

Dedicated to the beautiful and wonderful friend that asked me to write something on this topic for her. Thank you for helping push me to write what became one of my favourite stories.

Flashback

"Like a bull in an antique shop, that one."

"I don't know how Julia does it... I couldn't handle such a clumsy little kid in my house."

"Tell me about it! I heard, from Jonathon, that just the other day she was in his shop. Buying another teapot."

"No!"

"It's true. That little devil of hers 'accidentally' broke the last one to smithereens. Get this, he wasn't even pouring tea!"

"What? What was he doing?"

"Apparently, Julia says he told her that he wanted to surprise her with a clean house."

"So, he was washing it?"

"No! He was mopping the floor! Got me as to how he managed to knock a teapot that was out of his reach, right off the wall but he did!"

"Oh my god... Well, did you hear how just last week the little Williams kid ran home to his parents with a black eye and split lip? Apparently, he ran into that Anton. Rather, Anton ran into him."

"Aiiishhh poor kid didn't stand a chance."

"Nope. Went to shake hands and somehow the book Anton was holding shot right out of his hand in his excitement, split the boy's lip, and when he jumped to help... Well, I'm sure you can imagine. Surprised that Williams boy isn't blind, with how hard Anton hit their heads together."

"And then there's that Daniels kid. Did you know, when the Daniels' moved here, the kid was sent to the hospital not 4 hours later?Yeah,Juliawenttogreetthem.Broughtthelittledisaster. Hugged the boy so hard his ribs fractured."

tongue click

"Disaster indeed. He needs to just stop touching people altogether, if he can't figure out how to do it without breaking something. One of these days, he's gonna kill someone."

"Mm. Maybe he'd be better off in a home, or something. You know, somewhere they could watch him. Keep him away from people..."

Anton, just 7 years old at the time, cowered against the wall, knees pulled to his chin, as he listened to the two old ladies talking about him. They were right. He was a disaster. He broke things all the time, just like he broke his parents. And, maybe he *would* kill someone accidentally.

Like that goldfish he tried to bring home to his mom last year, to surprise her because she said she loved them while they were at the fair one day. So he found a man selling them, proudly saved his allowance, and bought one. On the way home, a truck startled him and he jumped, the little bag with the precious little fish in it, falling to the ground. Rolled away from him, right into the street. He dashed towards it, forgetting to look for traffic, and froze when he saw headlights coming at him. When he caught up with his mindfinally,andunclenchedhisbody,thebaghadexplodedon the asphalt... He tried, desperately, to get to it and rescue it. Tried to gingerly pick it up, carrying it in his shirt all the way home as he ran.

But it was too late. Anton lied and said he lost his allowance on the way to school that week, instead of telling her about the fish he buried in the yard. And he lied again when she asked about that turned soil, saying he saw a chipmunk or something out there.

☞ ☜

The final straw came when Anton was about 12. The day he decided the risk of accidental harm wasn't worth... Anything. Not when the risk of harm was so great around Anton. His mom was sick, so sick she had to stay home. She was weak, unable to cook their dinner, so Anton offered.

He was careful as he set up the ingredients. Careful as he cut the vegetables. Careful even as he gently placed the plates on the table. The table he stubbed his toe on, and let out a loud hiss of pain, but continued nonetheless, because his mom was hungry, and counting on him for food. She heard his pain, though, and came around the corner to check on him. When he turned, pot of hot tomato soup in his hands, he ran right into her. The entire pot of stew landed all over the front of her, down her legs, and pooled with an incriminating red at her feet.

He panicked, dropped the pot and reached out for his mom, but she pedaled backwards gasping.

Once they got to the hospital, Anton kicked his feet anxiously in the waiting room. Was she okay? All the red was just the tomatoes, right?

Anton's thoughts spiraled back to what the old ladies said. "One of these days, he's gonna kill someone"

He would. He would and he'd have no way of stopping it, unless he could stop it before it happened. But how? He's been so careful. He does things slowly, he thinks out a plan for what to do before he does it, step by step. He doesn't work out, he eats less food, he tries to be weak and still...

Still, he hurts people. Just being around him is enough to get hurt, and touching him means being hurt for sure...

"Young man? You're Anton Phillips, right? You're here with your mother?"

Anton jumps upright, bending too quickly to bow and promptly smacks right into the doctor's hand, sending his clipboard clattering to the ground.

"Oh! I'm sorry, I'm so sorry, I'm so-"

"Now now, it's fine, it's just a clipboard." The doctor places a hand on his shoulder and squeezes it gently.

'This time, it's just a clipboard' Anton thinks, shoulders slumping in defeat.

"So, your mother is... Well she's fine. She will be, she just needs a little time to heal is all. Would you like to see her?"

Anton swallows hard, and nods. "Please, if that's okay"

"Of course! You're her son, after all. So, just to warn you, she is bandaged quite a bit right now, and she has a brace on one foot. But she'll be alright in a few weeks!"

"Br-Brace? W... why?"

"Ah, well we were bandaging her burns and noticed some bruising on one of her feet. After an x-ray we realized the bones in that foot had a couple hairline fractures. An almost-break, so the brace is more preventative than anything. Just while those heal up a bit."

Anton slumps even further. Of course he broke his mother's foot. Of course he burned her whole body. He could have killed her just trying to put food on the table, what if he tries to hug her and punctures a lung? What if he tries to kiss her and he knocks her over and she falls and hits her head and-

"Here we are. Go on in, she is awake." The doctor leaves with a kind smile, gesturing into the room his mother is in.

Stepping gingerly into the room, teenage Anton flicks his eyes left and right, looking for obstacles. Potential hazards. Anything at all that might cause a problem. He side steps the coat rack carefully, eyeing it like it has limbs that will grab at him. He starts to sit in the chair by the bed, hesitating, before scooting it a few feet back. Safely away from his bed-bound mother, who looked like a last-minute mummy in a very bad play, with a thick black boot looking thing on her left leg. His eyes well with unshed tears, shoulders shaking softly as his anxiety quakes within him. He could have killed her. His poor single mother, alone because of him, working long hours because of him, paying other kids' medical bills because of him...

She could have died because of him too.

He can't even fathom the 'what if' situation or question what he would do if that happened. Because he's stuck on that single line. She could have died and it would have been his fault.

Julia reaches out to hold his hands, but he jerks away quickly.

"I... Mom please, I don't... I don't want to hurt you. Please... I'm so sorry mom I'm sorry I'm-" He chokes, a sob wracking through his (big) little frame. Her heart aches in response for him, but she nods.

"Darling it was an accident. You know that, yes? I startled you, and it was an accident. It's alright honey it's okay, yeah?"

Anton shakes his head. 'It's not okay' he wants to say 'It's not okay and it'll never be okay'

He just whimpers, arms wrapping around his legs as he pulls his knees to his chest again, and rocks. He rocks himself, and hugs himself, and yearns for a life where he could be normal. Where he could make friends, and hug his father, and make soup for his sick mother.

5 years later, Graduation day

"You did it, my sweet... Congratulations darling. I'm proud of you." Julia croons for her only son as she watches from a chair while he dons his graduation jacket. She aches to reach forward and straighten his tie, but settles for pointing it out to him with a smile.

"Ah, thanks mom! How's this?" He adjusts and turns so she can see him directly, and not through the mirror.

"Beautiful. You're so beautiful son." Her eyes well a little as she thinks of the journey he's made, as well as the one he's yet to begin.

An hour later, and they're at the ceremony. Anton walks incredibly slow, in shoes that are a little too small, and clothes that are tailored to be as fitted as possible. He keeps his jacket buttoned the entire time, and sits straight, stiff, awaiting the ceremony start. He's hyper aware of the throng of people all around him, adjusting his stance to ensure no one touches him. Or, more specifically, he touches no one. He keeps glancing around, a habit he developed acutely in high school, to accommodate the large amounts of people around him all the time.

So, it's no surprise when he catches the glances of people that clearly know his seat-mates. He stands carefully and steps over, offering his seat with a slow and measured half bow.

"Would you like this seat?"

The fellow graduate-to-be eagerly jumps over and into his vacated chair, scooting it against their friend in their haste.

Anton can't stop the sour little huff as he thinks, 'If I'd done that, the little bump probably would have cut off a finger...'

Eyes darting, he spots a chair on the end of the row that's empty, and carefully sits down. It makes him a little anxious to be so near to the main aisle, where everyone will be walking, but he reasons now at least he only has one seat-mate and not two to worry about. The ceremony goes about as one expects. Anton is hyper-vigilant every second, is slow and steady as he accepts his certificate of graduation, carefully accepts a small bundle of flowers ensuring no fingers are touched, and opts for a deep bow instead of a hand shake. Maybe the staff thinks he's deeply respectful... But that's better than thinking he's rude, and it's certainly better than them getting hurt.

His mind flashes with imagery of 'what if' situations. Where he touches a hand accepting the certificate and the man handing it over topples forward, right off the stage, and then black out, and the next thing you know he's just not breathing. Or, Anton trips walking across the stage, lands on the seated staff members, crushes all the flowers, sticks thorns in the staff as he tries to get up, and then they'll probably get infected and be hospitalized or WORSE. He shakes his head lightly and smiles, bowing to the student body, before stepping carefully, gently, softly, down the stairs off the stage. He stands adjacent to the line of students getting pictures taken, but makes sure he's 3 steps back. Just in case.

His mom rushes down to photograph him, and he tries to ignore the sad smile she gives... And the weird looks the other families give the two of them. Because, unlike everyone else there is no celebratory hug, no proud embrace, no firm shaking of hands. There's a quiet exchange of smiles, a few tears, and a lot of hand gestures that are more to soothe his mother's eagerness and nerves than actually guiding anything.

"I'm proud of you, Tony. You know that, I hope? I love you so much, and I'm so proud of you."

Anton nods and looks away, body aching to hold his mother and soothe her almost as much as his heart aches to be held. Swallowing thickly, he forces a wide grin, dimples on display.

"I know mom. I know... I love you too, more than you could know..." He whispers the last half to himself as he poses for one more picture.

Present day, age 22

Anton liked to think that over the years, he'd gotten better. Better about watching his step, better about not hurting people, better about being aware of things around him in general. He was, predictably, a top student at the university, excelling in every subject he had. Funny how much time you have to dedicate to studying when you don't have friends that act as distractions. Or any kind of social or romantic interest at all. Or extracurriculars that involve other people.

To get his extracurricular credits, Anton had chosen to take up photography and botany with a side of museum loitering in his free time. Photography tended to get crowded if you had people, and only one person could be in the red room at a time. Botany required absolutely no human contact, and Anton had quickly learned which plants died under his hands and which ones thrived. He needed ones that didn't have delicate foliage but they could require special care, that was fine.

He was clumsy, but not forgetful.

At least, he hadn't ordinarily been forgetful. Today, though, he had somehow mixed up his alarm clock with AM and PM, and so he had missed his first two classes. His first ever no-show, and he had only himself to blame for buying a stupid 24 hour alarm clock.

For the aesthetic of it.

He rolls his eyes at himself in the mirror, jabbing at it with a finger and leaning in.

"You are an idiot. A late idiot, who has to rush to the third class of the day to at least get one in. Idiot."

Dashing around his room, he stubbed his toes no less than thrice, twice on the same foot, and smacked his head into the corner of his desk as he bent down to grab his backpack. He's pretty sure he has a papercut somewhere, but definitely does not want to stop and figure it out. He just wipes his hand until he doesn't feel moisture, and keeps going, rushing out of his dorm room as fast as he can. He does make sure he hears his door click shut, at least, so he doesn't worry about coming back to anything being stolen.

Feeling a spark of gratitude for the hour of the day, he sprints down the very empty halls, climbs stairs three at a time, and swings around the rails letting his large frame's momentum propel him forward. It's little wonder, with the laws of physics, that the very large Anton-object in motion... Would tend to stay in motion... Even if it collided with another object, especially if that object were smaller in mass. So, gripping a sturdy metal railing, Anton swings around the final set of stairs and immediately starts jogging around the corner... And grunts as he feels a small weight thump against his chest and belly, head knocking something hard on the way.

"Fuck!"

Anton grunts, and looks up with wide eyes at what he hit.

Who he hit.

It takes a minute to sink in that he hit someone, and it takes only a second more for absolute panic to set in. He HIT SOMEONE.

"S-s-sorr-sorry I- Sor- I di- Sh- S-so" He stutters out as much of an apology as he can through chattering teeth. His body, while large, is severely undernourished, and as panic sets in so does the cold. He shakes with it, eyes wide and pupils dilated.

He gasps when the small man in front of him grins at him, dusting off his arms dramatically. Because his teeth are pink. Pink with blood.

"B-blood... sorr-sorry I di- you're -I c-can't S-sorry"

"Hey hey it's okay big guy I'm fine. You're late, and I'm not even supposed to be here. My fault. I'm fine though, see?" He gestures at himself, kicking his legs out to show they aren't broken.

"No harm, no foul. Here lemme help you up-"

"NO" Anton shrieks and kicks himself backwards, scrambling over his spilled books and papers, until his back presses to the wall.

"D-do-don't- Don't c-come- N-no t-touch Ple-ease" He grinds out through clenched teeth.

The man looks at him with concern and leans up with hands raised. "Okay, you don't want me to touch you, right?"

Anton nods frantically, knees pulled up to his chin, fighting the urge to rock himself too.

"Okay... Okay I won't touch. Can I pick up your books for you?"

"S-s-okay I c-can"

The man shakes his head, and scoots back a little to start grabbing them.

"You stay right there buddy okay? Just stay there, and lean on the wall. Let me get this yeah? Hey, look at my eyes real quick. Breathe in with me, okay? In... And out... I'm going to get these books, you keep that breathing okay? And keep looking at me"

Cyrus slowly picks up the books, one at a time, and neatly piles them back into Anton's backpack. He takes care to neatly stack the papers and put them all in together, sandwiched between two books to make sure they didn't get bent.

Then, he grabs his own things, scribbling on a piece of paper before scooting slowly back to Anton.

"Okay, here's your bag" He pushes Anton's bag beside him, eyes locked on the bigger man's and continues "And here's my number. Just text me if you're missing something, or something is broken or... idk, if you feel sick or something. I'll help, okay? Let me help."

He sticks the paper on top of Anton's bag before standing and slinging his own back over one shoulder. As Anton stands with him and cowers a little, the man reaches out to pat him on the arm reassuringly, out of habit. Anton flinches again, heart dropping to his stomach, and a choking sound is all that can be heard as he stumbles back again until his back and heels kick the wall.

"Shit! Sorry, sorry that was- It's habit I- Fuck." The man runs a handthroughhishairandpincheshislipstogether. "I'mreally sorry about that. Please, don't hesitate to text or call if you need something, yeah? I'll... I'll try not to touch you again okay?"

Heart pounding in his chest, Anton can only stare dumbly with eyes blown wide and round.

The man sighs, shoulders drooping, before turning and walking calmly down the stairs.

Anton slowly shuffles to his scheduled class, hugging the walls tightly along the way. He sits quietly in the farthest table he can reach, away from the door, away from the aisle, and takes exactly 0 notes for the first time ever. Because, sitting in that class, all he could think about was the burning heat on his arm. Was that man a wizard? How and why was Anton's arm still... weighed down? And warm? And tingling?

When the professor called his name to get his attention, his voice was hoarse and scratchy as he called back, "Yes sir?"

The professor must have noticed, because he mumbled something about "Being sick" and "Understandable then" and called on someone else.

When the class was over, Anton folded up his blank notebook, capped his pen carefully, slid both into their respective compartments, and walked slowly back to his dorm room. He felt like he was in a daze, like he was watching his own body move, from outside of it. As he stood by his dorm room, it took a few minutes for him to catch up to the fact that he had to unlock his door.

"Where are... I had them, they shou- Oh no..."

He frowned, and then frantically patted every pocket he had. Dumping out the contents of his backpack, he rummaged through every single item before slumping to the ground in pure defeat.

"My keys..." He whispered, head falling forward to *clunk* against the heavy wooden door.

Cyrus stalked down the dorm hallway after his own classes had finished, sweating profusely. It was a long walk in un-air-conditioned plazas to get from his last class today back to his dorm. He was practically salivating at the prospect of a nice cool shower. Turning last minute down the adjacent hallway, to check on the showers capacity, he tripped over something and brought a hand out to catch himself. With a gasp, he realized this was the same man from before.

Curled against the doorframe, hugging himself, he looked like he'd made a nest of all his belongings and passed out in the middle of it. Cyrus smiled, endeared, before frowning. What are the odds he'd fall, twice in the same day, over the same man? And, more importantly, why was this man nesting on his belongings in the hallway? Cyrus reached up to the door and twisted the handle, frown growing as he realized it was locked.

"Ahh... Poor guy, today wasn't your day, was it?" Cyrus whispered, reaching out to pat his arm before jerking back seconds away from contact. "Shit, right, no touching."

Cyrus hums softly, then stands and jogs to his room. When he comes back, tools in hand, he smiles at the still-sleeping form on the floor. 'He's quirky, but cute' he thought to himself as he quietly shimmied a bookmark (The best tool ever, if you asked Cyrus) in the lock. A second later, the soft click echoed in the quiet hallway as the door popped open. Cyrus reached back and made sure the lock was twisted to the open position before squatting down and quietly gathering the man's things. For the second time, at that. He was gingerly tugging a folder from beneath Anton's body, careful not to touch him as was requested, when Anton awoke with a start. His body jerked, and on reflex Cyrus reached a hand out to cushion the impact of Anton's head against the doorframe.

"Easy tiger, I'm trying not to touch you okay? Just... Noticed your door was locked, got it open for you... I didn't touch anything but the handle, and um... Here, I can sanitize these if you want? I have sanitizer on me" He says, voice low and gentle.

He figures the man's aversion to touch is probably because he's a germaphobe, which Cyrus understands. Especially in this post-pandemic era.

"S-sanitizer?" Anton says slowly.

"Yeah ah... I'm sorry, I touched these things without asking... I'm sorry. You know, for future reference, this kind of thing is totally okay to text me about, yeah? I meant it when I said, you know, if you need anything... Or, if you just wanna talk."

Cyrus waves a little, hand close to his body, and smiles. "Nice to see you again by the way. If you ever get locked out again, I'm down the hall, last door on the right. Come get me, okay?"

He looks at the wide-eyed man as he stands, slowly offering a hand out. "Would you like help up? If not it's okay! I won't touch you, I swear"

Anton slowly reaches a hand to the side of his head, where the back of Cyrus's had had briefly touched it. A squeaky sound hissed out of his mouth as his throat constricted. His head felt warm, fuzzy all over, and his heart was pounding in his chest.

"No! N-no please don't... touch. I'll hurt you."

Cyrus jerked his hands to his body, lips thinning. "Look, I did apologize, you don't have to threaten me or anything... I'm not... I tried not to touch you, I respect your wishes okay?"

"And" He continued, stepping back a little, "If I did something to offend you, I'm really sorry, okay?"

Anton's brows furrowed in confusion. "Threat-No! No no!" As he rushed to stand up, the blood rushed to his long legs, sending him tipping forward with dizziness. Cyrus's arms reached out to catch him, hands landing on Anton's broad chest as he did so.

He could feel the erratic pulse beating through him, and held still, waiting for Anton to make the next move. After a moment, when nothing happened, he inhaled and softly spoke.

"I'm beginning to think either the Universe has a thing for us falling over each other, or you actually really want me to touch you after all... Which is it big guy?"

As he spoke, his warm breath ghosted across Anton's neck, sending goosebumps down his arms. His heart, already beating out of his chest, seemed to simultaneously fall out of his stomach. Suddenly his lungs couldn't get enough air, and the air they did... Anton inhaled slowly before scrambling backwards, the scent of oranges and musk pervading his nose. He darted his eyes around Cyrus, looking for injuries, before stumbling over yet another apology.

"I-I'm not threat... I don't... I don't want to h-hurt you. Just... just... people get hurt y-you know? Sorry... I'm sorry... And thank you! Definitely... thank you..."

Flooded with a sudden flush in his cheeks, Anton looked away and tried to bow awkwardly. His chest and head were tingling, he felt even dizzier than when he stood up, and now he was just making things weird. He had to leave before he hurt him...

"Thanks. Thank you. For this, and, you know, earlier... and... yeah bye"

He turned, bolted into his room and locked the door, slumping to the floor beside it, heart thumping.

On the other side, Cyrus chuckled to himself, staring at the forgotten folder still on the floor.

"Cute" He whispered before pushing the folder under the door's crack.

Anton strains his ears to listen for Cyrus's footsteps fading down the hall before exhaling loudly a breath held for entirely too long. He can feel his neck twitching with his pulse, bringing a hand up to it carefully to feel the *thump thu-thump thu-thump*

He turns his head to look at the folder that was pushed under the door, and inhales a measured breath.

"That was... a lot. That was a lot. He's okay though, right? And... I'm okay, I think..."

Getting up, he moves to his bed and sits on it, hands on his knees, staring at the floor.

"Okay Anton. You're okay. Everything is okay. He didn't get hurt, so maybe... Maybe he just didn't touch you long enough. Is that it? Is there a time limit on how long it's necessary?"

His hands trail up his body, landing on his chest. "He touched me... Why... why can I still..."

Anton's eyes close as he focuses on the thick feeling on his chest, where Cyrus's hands rested. He can still feel them, as he rests his own on top of those spots. He can feel the long fingers, warm against his shirt. Is his shirt still warm from the touch? He slides one hand up to his head, cradling the spot where the back of Cyrus's hand touched it. He thinks he can feel the touch there, too, but it's gentler. Like Cyrus is caressing his head. Anton's heart clenches in an icy grip as he imagines it. Imagines, as he leans back on his bed, what it would feel like to have someone care about you enough to hold you. To have someone wrap their arms around you, warm and strong, unafraid of harm coming their way. To hold them back, with love and affection and not an inkling of fear of harming them.

"What would I do?" He muses aloud. "I would... I would stroke their face, I think..."

He strokes his own cheek, imagines doing that to someone else. The person's face is blank, but Anton doesn't dwell. He shifts, imagining someone else touching his face that way.

This time, a face does appear. He jerks upright, face flushing warm, heart beating out of his chest once more.

"...what?" He whispers to no one, as usual.

A very confused Anton finally falls asleep about 3 hours before his first class in the morning. Determined not to be late this time, he triple checked his fancy new clock's alarm and set four different ones on his phone.

"Not today" he whispered before crawling into bed.

So it's no surprise, when he finally does pull his eyelids open with both hands and a bowl of icy water, that he is functioning at maybe 20% of his usual brain power. But, he gets out the door, he remembers his keys, and he has his backpack. Everything important. He starts trudging down the hall, blinking sleep from his eyes, hugging the walls as he usually did at busy times. His arms were shoved deep into his pockets, elbows locked, making himself as small as he could at his stature.

His first class goes about as expected. That is to say, he doesn't remember a damn thing that happens. His second and third, much the same, but he at least took notes, if the ink smudges all over his shirt are anything to go by. It's the fourth class, ordinarily one of his favourites, that he realizes the day isn't goingsmoothly.Becausenow,Antonisawareofsomeoneelsein the school. Someone whose hands he can close his eyes and feel on his body. And apparently, that someone is in his class.

'Has he always been there? Did I never notice him? Why would I, I don't look for people. So is it just that, then? That I know what he looks like now, so I am seeing him?'

As he watches Cyrus, he barely blinks. It's not until Cyrus looks back at him, and smiles, waving his hand a little, that Anton registers he's been staring. His eyes dart down to Cyrus's hand, and then he's staring at that, eyes un-focusing. Or focusing? All he can see is fingers, and smooth, pale skin.

And just like that, his chest heats up, blood rushing through his body. He can feel it, all of Cyrus's body pressed against his as they ran into each other the first time. He can feel the fingers on his chest, the smooth skin on his head. Anton feels a deep ache, one he gave up years ago. He yearns to feel touch again. Not that it ever went away, but he'd accepted long ago that he just wouldn't feel it anymore. And once he resigned himself to that truth, things got easier. It just... fell off his radar as something he wanted. Something he needed.

Until now. Until that man. What was his name again?

Anton breaks his stare to rummage through his bag, unaware of how loudly he was doing so.

"Anton Phillips! Will you please either search quietly, or wait until I am finished speaking to do so?"

"Ah! Y-Yes professor, I'm so sorry!" Anton jerks upright, hands in his lap, elbows tucked at his sides. His eyes dart over to Cyrus just in time to see Cyrus writing something down in large letters.

As he holds the paper up, Anton blushes.

"U R Anton?"

Anton's mouth went dry, but he nodded slowly, and then Cyrus was scribbling something else.

"Hungry?"

When he hesitated, Cyrus scribbled rapidly again, scratching out the old letters, and held up the paper once more.

"No touch"

Cyrus mimes crossing his heart and smiles broadly at him. He mouths a word, but Anton can't see it through the mist welling in his vision. He nods at Cyrus anyway, uncaps a pen and writes a reply.

"Food 👍"

Cyrus's grin as he returns to his work is infectious, Anton shyly smiling to his own paper as he bends his head for the rest of the class.

"Hey big guy"

"H-hi... I'm sorry, I forgot your name... And I lost the paper..." Anton looked at his hands sheepishly, embarrassed to present himself like such a fuck up already.

Instead of judgment, Cyrus just grins a wide, gummy smile and holds out his hand expectantly.

"Phone?"

Anton quickly pulls his phone out of his two-sizes-too-small pants and fumbles it on the hem, dropping it to the ground. He bends and apologizes quickly, standing up slowly to ensure he doesn't knock Cyrus out like he did the Williams kid all those years ago.

"Sorry, sorry... I'm..."

"A big guy?" Cyrus huffs a little amused chuckle "Yeah, I noticed. S'okay Anton. I'm Cyrus by the way. Cyrus Matthews. I'd shake your hand, but... It's fine. A bow, then?"

"Y-yeah, sure." Anton bows his upper body slowly, careful to angle a little to the side to clear Cyrus's range of motion. "Nice to meet you... C-Cyrus Matthews"

"How old are you?"

"Ah, um, 22... You?"

"Oh! I'm 23. You can talk more comfortably, if you'd like!"

Anton looked up, eyes wide. "Oh? Are you um... Sure? We just met, and... And you might not want me to-"

"Hey" Cyrus holds a hand out and gestures at Anton, holding a finger out "Stop that. I wanna be your friend. If you don't wanna be mine, that's okay... but... I'm gonna keep trying to be yours. So. Take it or leave it but either way you're getting it."

"Yes, um... Cyrus" Anton bows his head politely, clutching at the phone as it's returned to him with a new contact added.

The second contact in his phone.

Anton doesn't have time to dwell on that thought, though, because immediately Cyrus is tugging at his sleeve to get him to walk. Figuratively speaking, that is.

"Hey Anton? If you don't wanna go today, we can go tomorrow? Oh, or do you have another class this evening?"

Jerking to the present, Anton's heart thumps erratically in his chest.

"Ah! Uh, no, no class. Today is good, yeah... today..."

"Soo... What's your favourite food?" Cyrus asks, slinging his bag over one shoulder and walking into the bustling hallway.

"Uh, I like anything really. 'Cept seafood..."

"No seafood? Really?"

Anton smiles and mimics, in English, "Fish are friends, not food"

"Okay Bruce" Cyrus replies, laughing. "So, no seafood, no touching, what else should a friend know about you?"

The brief laughter on Anton's face freezes, and falls for a moment. What should friends know about you? What do you say to a friend? How... How do you have friends? Do you just say you're friends? What... How?"

Cyrus stops walking, eyes wide, and stares at Anton incredulously.

"You... You have never had a friend?" He asks, slowly, careful not to sound judgmental.

Anton realizes a breath too late he said those thoughts out loud, and turns slowly with his eyes squeezed shut in embarrassment.

"I... Um... Well, no, not really... no..."

"...oh. Ohhhh..." Cyrus exhales, things making a little more sense now. "Right, well, I'm not a very high maintenance friend, so it's a good thing you have me now! You can practice on me before you go running off with all the new friends you're gonna make!"

And then, they're walking again. No questions, no judgmental looks and no pity etched all over his face.

Anton is deep in thought, feet walking with sheer muscle memory, right to his dorm door. Cyrus waits patiently as Anton dumps his bag and grabs his wallet and ID. He pats his body, checking for keys and anything else he's missing, and Cyrus just... observes. Takes in the habitual behaviours. He notes everything he sees, right down to the clear discomfort hidden away on Anton's face, and the way his clothes cling to him almost as tightly as his limbs do as he walks. He glances away, though, when Anton trips on a book and sends it flying under the bed, the sound of something crashing distantly.

Flushing pink, Anton chooses to ignore it and quickly steps up to the door, clearing his throat. "Okay uh, Cyrus, I'm ready. S-sorry it took so long..."

"So you are! C'mon I know a great place that's not far from campus."

Anton locks his door and lets it click closed, following a few steps behind Cyrus to make sure he doesn't accidentally trip on him. Cyrus, however, slows his pace to walk side by side.

"You know, if you don't want us to fall over top of each other, again, we should walk side by side. Then, if we do start to fall, the other can catch us, yeah?"

He doesn't look over at Anton as he speaks, just reads his mind somehow and Anton thinks that's incredible. How does he do that?

As he ponders this thought, he doesn't watch his surroundings like he normally would. Not until he feels the body heat of Cyrus pressing dangerously close to him as the smaller man's arms spread protectively in a cage around him. People are pushing in the hall due to some commotion that he can't see, that he didn't notice, but Cyrus did. And Cyrus is now protecting him from being pushed. His heart leaps in his chest at the thought of this little man trying to protect him. Him, whom he barely knows, and who's already hurt him once. Once they pass the commotion, Cyrus silently returns to normal distance at Anton's side. He opens the campus door and holds it open for Anton to pass through, unobstructed. There is a calmness between them, that fills the silence with meaning. It's comfortable, this kind of silence.

Anton wonders if all friendships are this easy. This feels so easy, that Anton questions all his previous attempts at friendship. Why did they all end so spectacularly before they even got started? He stops walking suddenly, realization coming to him. Because he stopped. He ended them. Every single first attempt at friendship resulted in Anton hurting the other person. After he hurt them, he distanced himself and they... accepted that. It felt like the normal way to do things so he never questioned it. Why would they want to befriend someone who hurts them?

But Cyrus... Cyrus came back that same day. And then again. And now, here they are, walking in comfortable silence.

"You okay big guy?" Cyrus turns, tilts his head questioningly at Anton.

"You're... really my friend?"

"Of course I am, I said I was, right?"

"Why?"

Cyrus jerks back a little, face scrunched up. "Do I... need a reason?You'renice,you'reinteresting,Iwanttoknowmoreabout   you, so... we're friends. Yeah?"

Anton frowns, puzzled. Cyrus shrugs and turns, walking again with his hands comfortably in his pockets. "Come on friend! I can practically smell the hot dogs cooking from here!"

When they arrive at the little street stall, Cyrus claims a table in the corner of the tent, so Anton is far away from the main walk paths. He immediately sits in the opposing chair, and orders a heaping plate of fresh fries.

"You absolutely don't have to say anything you aren't comfortable with it, but... I was wondering if I could ask what the touch thing is about?" Cyrus rushes to finish the thought, hands up defensively, "No no not because of anything bad! I just... I thought maybe you were a germaphobe?"

Cyrus hums, chewing on a new fry. "But then, you don't seem to sanitize anything you touch, or even go out of your way to not touch things. As far as I can see, it's just people?"

Swallowing, he continues, taking Anton's silence as defensive. "Again, you don't have to tell me anything okay? If it's something I can do to avoid, or help make you more comfortable... I'd like to, you know? Just... Not touching is fine, nevermind..."

Anton, who sat frozen with the first fry halfway to his mouth, swallows his spit and gently puts the food down.

"It's... I hurt people... When... When I touch them. Or just, being around them. Being my friend means getting hurt. Being anything to me means being hurt, and the closer you are..." He pinches his lips together with a sour expression "The worse it is..."

Cyrus chews, quiet for a minute. Two minutes. It's stretching into three and Anton is nervous, not sure what this silence means. So his thoughts take over, again.

'Is he regretting it? Is he adding up all the times he's been hurt? Fuck, there's been more than one time hasn't there? Oh god what if I reach for that bottle of sauce and I flip the food onto him and he gets hot oil and fries all in his lap and then he'll be burned AND THEN-'

"You want the last piece?" Cyrus nonchalantly holds the final chunk of potato between his fingers, hovering towards Anton, whose head jerks up.

"Ah, um, if you... if you don't, I can... I can have it yeah..."

Silence settles between them again, but Cyrus doesn't seem to Anton to be upset. More like... More like he's ignoring the cause for the silence. Like it never existed. Like he never asked a question that went unanswered. As Anton quietly finishes the last fries he has, he twists his fingers in his lap.

"Growing up I... I hurt people a lot. I didn't mean to, I swear I didn't!"

"I believe you, it's okay..." Cyrus reaches over the table, wanting to reassure Anton with a squeeze, but settles for grabbing his cup and refilling his drink for him. "Go on..." he says.

"Well, I... Nobody liked me much, once they found out about it. Kids either laughed at me, or feared me. There... There really wasn't an in-between. I'm just too big, and too clumsy. I break things around me, like some... some kind of destruction god... And, well... Nobody wants that around them..."

Cyrus is nodding, sipping his drink as he listens.

"Aren't you going to ask?" Anton says, fingers squeezing themselves to calm his nerves.

"What would you like me to ask?"

"Don't you... Don't you wanna know how I hurt them? How I'll p-probably hurt you?"

Cyrus shrugs. "Can't say I'm all that worried if I'm honest. That just sounds like life. We get hurt. It happens. If I avoided everything that could hurt me, I would be living in a bubble that doesn't exist. Literally everything has the potential for harm."

Anton stares, slack-jawed, as Cyrus continues.

"I mean, really. You can drown in two inches of water. Is it likely? Fuck no. But if you pass out and land in just enough water to cover your nose and mouth BAM you've drowned. Paper can slice between the web of your fingers. Windows can break. Food can burn. Hell, I've choked on my own spit."

"Talk about insulting... Your own body trying to choke itself with its own fluids!"

Cyrus laughs, and his smile is full of gums and teeth. Anton smiles softly, his own dimple showing briefly.

"Aww, cute. Look at that dimple!" Cyrus closes one eye and mimes poking the dimple with a finger held up, pretending he can touch it. The gesture is sweet, and Anton tries not to imagine that finger sliding against his dimple in reality.

"Look, all I'm saying is... I've come away with more injuries just living my daily life, than I have when I've come in contact with you these past days. And, sure, maybe you are some God of Destruction, you're certainly a strong presence after all. But, maybe I don't mind? Maybe I like that about you? And, hey, I suppose if nothing else, we could find you a job with a demolition crew eh?"

Cyrus turns to get some corndogs to go, saying he likes this lady's the most, and Anton thinks he catches a wink thrown his way.

And he certainly starts mentally chewing on everything Cyrus said. He should be adding those examples to the list of things he's anxious about doing, ways of causing harm to people. Instead...

Instead, he finds those words comforting him. Yeah, you could get hurt living your daily life. Yeah, you would have to live in a bubble to avoid getting hurt. Maybe... Maybe it wasn't so bad? Maybe he wasn't so bad?

The two of them walk side by side back to the dorms, down the halls and up to Anton's door. Cyrus looks like he wants to say something, but Anton is careful to avoid leaving an opening. He's tired, and he's afraid of oversharing if Cyrus pokes any further. Because sharing means caring, and caring means hurting. Cyrus smiles and gives a little wave, stepping backwards from Anton's doorway.

"So, I guess we'll part here? Kinda feel like I took you on a cheap date, walking you here and all..."

A blushing Anton grins cheekily and replies, softly, "I wouldn't know if it was a cheap date or not... Would just call it a good one."

Anton isn't prepared for the soft flush creeping up Cyrus's neck and ears at his words, just as Cyrus wasn't prepared for the heat gripping his chest at the implication of them.

"Ah, well, please... I hope you don't call this a date? If I... If I were to take you on one... you know... I um... It'd be nicer. That's all. Kay, see you later big guy" and then he's gone, bolting down the hall to his own room.

"Cute" Anton whispers, moments before Cyrus trips on an untied shoelace, causing Anton to gasp. He can't see if Cyrus falls or not, though, because a group of students pass between them at that precise moment. Anton stands on his tiptoes, hoping to see a shock of Cyrus's hair over the crowd...

But nothing. Cyrus is either too small to be seen over the crowd, or he's already darted into his own dorm. Anton's heart is heavy with concern and guilt.

'If he got hurt... Was it still my fault? Fuck, did I step on his shoe? Is that why a lace was undone?'

His thoughts start to spiral, until he remembers he has Cyrus's number.

Anton: Cyrus? It's Anton. Did you get to your room okay? I couldn't see you walk all the way, and I didn't know if you got hurt. If you did, I have ice? Or, bandages? Or um... I dunno... Sorry...

His phone vibrates in his hand almost immediately, and he grins as he reads the reply.

Cyrus: Ah, you saw that? Well, I did say my normal life gets me hurt more often... right? Hah.

Anton Frowns, because Cyrus didn't deny that he got hurt. In fact, he seemed to imply he did?

Anton: Hey... Did you get hurt?

The phone is silent for longer than necessary and Anton is already throwing his shoes back on and grabbing his keys by the time he feels it vibrate again. Jogging down the hall, he stops at the last door and inhales.

"You can do it Anton. You can do it." He inhales, exhales, inhales again and holds his breath as his knuckles make contact with the door.

Cyrus opens it with an arm behind his back, not looking at Anton.

"Hey-"

"I'm really okay Anton... I promise... See? No pain right?" He grins, but it doesn't reach his eyes. Anton frowns.

"Let me... Lemme see?"

Shoulder slumping, Cyrus nods and opens the door wide enough for Anton to come in. As soon as he does, he stops and freezes.

'Holy shit this place is asking for me to break every damn thing in it...'

There is a guitar on a stand just inside the door, several forms of electronic equipment littered across the tiny desk with a PC seated on the far wall, and is that a bottle of whiskey sitting on the table? With crystal glasses?

His jaw tenses, and he fights the hyperventilation that threatens to take hold of his lungs. Wiping his clammy hands on his pants, he whispers, "Ah, I'll stay here... so... if you could just..."

Cyrus rolls his eyes and moves to sit on his bed. Gently shoving the table away with a foot, he pats the bed next to him.

"Come. Sit."

"Look man, I really don't thi-"

"Sit, Anton, or you won't be able to see my wrist."

Anton shuts his mouth with an audible clack of teeth, and slowly shuffles towards the proffered seat, each step carefully orchestrated with full focus on his balance.

"One step... at a time... easy Anton..." He chants to himself softly.

He eases onto the bed, wincing as it creaks under his weight. His eyes are darting, rapidly, around the room, and Cyrus can't help but pinch his lips in a tight smile as he lifts his arm up and out in front of Anton, waving it gently.

"Here you go. See? I'm fine. Perfectly fine. Just a little tender is all."

"T-tender?" Anton's eyes jerk to Cyrus's wrist, taking in its condition, and colouring, and then to Cyrus's eyes in concern. "What happened? What did-How did-Are you-"

"Relax, I am fine! Really! So fine I'd let you hold my hand right now if you wanted okay so-"

"H-hold..." Anton's eyes dart back down, between their hands. "Hold your h-hand..."

"Do you... want to?"

Anton swallows hard, eyes flicking back an.d forth before his own hand reaches out, out, towards Cyrus's pinkened wrist that's probably sprained. His hand shakes gently as he lifts it, hovers over Cyrus's fingers.

Lips parted, he imagines he can feel the heat of Cyrus's hand in his own. Imagines the tiny little hand cradled, softly, within his own. Imagines rubbing a thumb on the skin, and imagines locking their fingers together. Imagines, finally, that wrist beneath his lips, kissing the injury better.

He jerks his hand away and sits up straight, shivering slightly. He could almost feel it. He's sure of it, he was so close to it he could feel the heat of the man beside him. So why did he feel so cold?

"N-no thank you. I ah... I... I'm glad you're okay. M'gonna go."

He stands, stiff as a robot, shuffles his feet across the room and rattles the handle a little in his flustered state as he opened the door.

Cyrus's arm slowly falls back down to the bed as the click of the door echoes in the room.

'He wants touch... He wants it, but he can't do it...” He flings his body backwards onto his bed and grins. 'He wants it. Someday... Someday I hope we can touch...'

Anton nearly slams his own door closed in his rush to enter his room, flinging himself face down on his bed.

'What was that? Why was it so cold and hot all at once? Am I sick?'

He lifts his hands and looks at them, watches the trembling subside, with wonder. He can't stop thinking of 'what if'. What if he had touched Cyrus. Would he have felt warm? Cold? Would he have trembled too, or would he have been strong, firm, safe? His hands fall to the bed, grasping at the sheets. He wonders how it would feel to grip Cyrus's sheets like this. Imagines it. Imagines Cyrus pushing him onto his own bed, hears it creaking in his mind as his big frame is pushed backwards. Pictures Cyrus hovering over him like he's not twice his size.

"Cy-" He whispers in real time, one hand sliding up to touch his face like he imagines Cyrus would. He thumbs at his dimple the way Cyrus surely would, fingers dipping down to his neck and jaw. He ghosts them across his skin, shivering as goosebumps break out all over. His thighs are tense, as his hips gently roll in tiny little subconscious circles, yearning to feel something, to have a purpose. His fingers trail down to his chest, palm pressing against the spot where Cyrus's once rested. He lets his hand warm the spot up again, imagines it's Cyrus instead. The little hip rolls get stronger, grinding his half-erection into the bed, sending tiny jolts of pleasure through his body. He groans, squeezing his hand a little, feeling his nipple firm up beneath his thumb.

"Cy...rus" He whispers, a little louder.

Both his hands now roam, one back to his face, one down, down to his belly. He slowly shifts his weight to allow his shirt to lift up as he slides his fingers across his skin, hips still rolling against the bed. He groans at the friction, cock rapidly swelling. His other hand is on his face, whispered touches along his jaw, his nose, his lips. They part with a gasp and his eyes flutter shut, the imaginary Cyrus in his mind becoming clearer. His rich voice coming together with fragments of things he said recently.

"Fuck... Anton... Aww, cute!"

"C-cute... Am I cute, Cyrus?"

"Yeah?... C'mon... Anton...Say my name..."

"Cyyyyy..."

        "Ohhh..." Imaginary Cyrus's voice is a whisper, an exhale, and Anton gasps as he imagines feeling the breath on his skin.

        He recalls Cyrus's hands on his chest, his breath against his cheek then, and groans.

"Fuck, Cy..."

His fingers grip his own chin, then, rough, and he gasps in shock.

"Cyrus!"

        His hips thrust into the bed, choking a moan out of his throat, his fingers squeezing harder on his chin once before sliding, down, to tentatively grasp at his throat. His mind starts down a trail of anxious thoughts, wondering if he would choke himself, pass out, be found dead in his room, so he moves his hand away quickly. No, not those thoughts. Cyrus wouldn't let him.

Cyrus.

Cyrus would touch him gently, carefully, with purpose. Yes, he'd hold Anton, he wouldn't just touch him. He'd lay his palm on Anton's cheek, thumbing at the crease of his eyes.

Like a lover.

Anton gasps again, hips bucking hard against the bed.

"Yes, that's it Cyrus… Lover… Love me… Please… fuck…"

He thrusts against the bed again, and again, chasing the friction until he can't take it anymore and flips himself over, awkwardly draping his limbs diagonally on his bed as he is. He sets a foot on the bed, lifts his hips, and shoves his pants down and off. With his lower hand, he roughly palms at his exposed cock, pressing it downwards, against a thigh. He keeps his eyes closed, imagines Cyrus there, mouthing at his skin. Imagines the wet heat pressing against his thigh, his hip, his belly.

That belly clenches at the thought. He slowly guides the upper hand to his mouth, slides a finger around the edge at the same time his lower hand slips two fingers around the base of his cock. He moves both in little circles, grinding them a little harder each time.

"Hnnnng" He moans, two fingers pressing into his mouth. Grasping at his cock, he squeezes tightly, imagining Cyrus caged over top of him, ready to take him into his mouth. He opens his own wide, slides his fingers in slowly, and thrusts them back and forth. With a groan, he bucks his hips into his other hand to the same speed. He imagines Cyrus's hands gripping at his thighs as he fucks his mouth... Then salivates at the thought of his mouth being full of Cyrus's own cock.

"Fuck... Cyrus please... please... Love me Hyung... Love me.... Ple-heeease"

Anton begs his imaginary hyung, loudly, uncaring just now of the volume. All he cares about, all he can focus on, is the imaginary touch of fingers not his own, ghosting across his skin. All he can hear, is the imaginary voice of one man groaning his name. He feels so safe as he imagines these touches.

So safe, so warm, so full of love and comfort, that he chants and pleads as he approaches his climax.

"Hyung... Cyrus-Hyung... Love me... Please l-love me... Love me Hyunnnng" He moans, throat gasping as he cums, wet heat splashing on his leg and over his hand. "

Panting, he sucks the drool off his fingers and brings them down to his chest again, letting them warm Cyrus's spot... The spot Cyrus had touched... The first touch in so many long, lonely years. It was his spot, now, that spot over his heart. Maybe under it too...

Cyrus sidles into Music Theory and waves with his wrapped hand at his friend Josh. Josh is a dance major, but the two bonded over a love of writing songs. They both like to rap in their free time, and music has always been their first love. Sitting on the piano bench, his usual spot, Cyrus grins as Josh comes bounding over. Always full of energy, that one.

"Cyrus-ahhhhhhh what did you do? I never see you hurt your hands, they're so precious" He grabs Cyrus's wrist and gently cradles it, petting it like it was an injured bunny in his arms. The pout on his lips is almost cute.

"Ah, it's nothing. Precaution really. Tripped over my shoes yesterday..."

"Your shoes, huh?" Josh grins and Cyrus rolls his eyes. He knows that grin.

"Yes, my shoes thank you."

"Mmm I don't believe you."

"I can tell. Why?"

"Ohhhhh I may have heard a little something coming from your hallway last night that certainly didn't sound like 'tripping over shoes'"

Cyrus frowns, now, genuinely confused. "What do you mean? I really did trip over my shoes. Landed on my wrist, sprained it a little bit from the angle. It's really fine but-"

Josh just lifts a single brow. "Oh? You sure? Because I was walking down the dorm, and just as I passed your hallway, I heard someone screaming your name in the THROES of PASSION"

He drapes an arm dramatically over his eyes and smirks.

"So, if that wasn't you, then... there is another Cyrus in your hall? Hmmm? 'Cyrusssss. please... Please Cyyyy-'"

Cyrus swats at him to shut him up, face blushing furiously. He knows he was alone last night. He didn't even drink, so he couldn't have blacked it out. But then...?

"Well, I was genuinely alone last night once Tony left. Which was-"

"Ohhh? And so the truth is revealed! Who is Tonyyyy is he who you had moaning your name??"

"Gah I told you Joshua. Nothing like that. There's no way, even if I DID want to."

"And do you? Want to? You do, don't you??"

Cyrus turns back to the piano, fingers trailing across the keys as he thinks. He doesn't press them, just trails down them and wonders if he'll ever get to do something like this with Anton.

After a minute or so of silence, Cyrus whispers, "You ever met someone that doesn't like touch? Er, no, more like... Avoids it?"

"Yeah, actually"

Expecting to hear a no, he whips his head around with wide eyes. "Yeah?!"

Josh nods matter-of-factly. "Yep, just the one tho. A kid I grew up with. Well, grew up around is more accurate. We had an... interesting first meeting. He seemed super sweet, really shy though. Nervous like a bunny or something."

Cyrus nods, twisting on the bench to face Josh fully, his whole attention on the man as he tells this story. "What did... what happened?Tellmeabouthim?"

"Mm, memories are a bit blurred, this was... what... almost 15 years ago probably. At least 12 or so. But, my family moved when I was young, you remember? Well, the day we moved into that new house, this nervous kid, built like a tree, comes over with his mom. I remember thinking how I didn't see a dad... And how sad that was. His mom looked overworked, and he looked... scared. Scared like something was gonna hurt him or something you know? We hugged, and I was super excited about making a new friend so soon. But... I felt a pop. Turns out, that dance injury from a few months back wasn't completely healed."

"Dance injury?" Cyrus interrupts.

"Mm. I'd been learning lifts at the time, and because I'm a boy they automatically wanted me to do the lifting. Despite the fact that I am very much built to be the one lifted instead... I had fractured a rib from the stress of the lifting."

"Whoa..."

"Yeah. Kid panicked, ran out, never saw him again. I was sad for a long time, because he was so sweet you know? Thought I made a friend already, just a day into my new home... But, I found out later why he never did..."

"Why?"

"Apparently, my parents shifted the blame for the injury onto him. Guilt-tripped his mom into paying the medical bills for it. She never questioned it, either. I found a bunch of letters my parents never opened. Apparently, every time she sent money, she wrote one."

"What did she say?"

"She apologized. Like, profusely. Almost groveled, lamented the 'pain and suffering your poor baby is going through at the hands of my own' and some other stuff. Sounded kinda like he hurt people often and she had to pay for it, but..."

"But what?" Cyrus presses, seeing the confliction on Josh's face.

"But, that just... doesn't match the kid I met, you know? He was terrified of... I dunno, literally everything. Whenever I saw him in school he sat away from everyone. Never engaged, never touched anyone, flinched if anyone came near him..." Josh shrugs. "I just... can't see that boy hurting anyone, let alone multiple people"

"What... what was his name? Do you remember?"

"Mmm... I don't think I knew his full name. He introduced him self as Ant though? But I think his mom called him something else.Moon? Toon?"

"Tony..." Cyrus whispers.

"Yeah that's it! Wait, what was this friend of yours' name again actually?"

Cyrus is breathless, as he pulls Josh to his feet. "We're leaving"

"Where are we-" Josh is yanked out of the room and down the grass towards the dorms, tugged firmly by Cyrus's deceptively strong frame.

Josh catches where they're headed as they round the plaza corner and Cyrus's dorm comes into view, so he jogs to catch up and step into stride with his friend.

"So *huff* you think *huff* your friend *huff* is also my *huff* childhood friend?"

"I don't think... I mean I do think... But I think I know." Cyrus stops suddenly, spinning to face Josh.

"Look. I made this friend. I dunno what possessed me to do it but… One minute I'm spying on Professor Phillips, the next minute, as you say, a 'tree of a man' rounds the corner and slams right into me. Ordinarily one should be mad, right? But I… I couldn't. I'm pretty sure he gave me a bloody nose or lip or something but I just couldn't be mad. He looked…"

"Pathetic?"

Cyrus winces. "I wouldn't… say that… but yeah, you get it. I just… I wanted to help him. Make him feel better. But the second I tried to touch him, he freaked out. And every time since then, it's gotten more and more clear why"

"Why?" Josh asks, as they slowly stroll again towards the dorms.

"He thinks he's going to hurt me. That… That somehow just being in the same vicinity as him is like handing over some kind of death warrant or something. Like you sign a contract admitting you will eventually get hurt by him and that… I… It…"

Cyrus sighs. "It breaks my fucking heart, Josh. And now, now I-"

"You like him" Josh states. It's not a question. He can see it all over Cyrus's face, he's fallen for the man already.

Cyrus doesn't answer, just marches purposefully to their hallway, hesitating with his hand over the door. Should he knock? Fuck, he should have texted first…

Bringing his hand down, he taps his phone to wake it up until the loud sound of knocking startles him.

"Yahhh! Josh!"

He gets a shrug in reply, and then the door is opening.

And Anton clearly just got back from the showers, because he's still dripping water as he stands there with a towel to his hair and his shirt very much missing. Cyrus's eyes start at his exposed belly and follow the trickling water up to the shimmering neck. His arms are surprisingly well defined, as one flexes with the towel on his hair. By the time their eyes meet, entirely too long has passed and now it's awkward...

"Hi! I'm Josh! Cyrus here thinks you might know me?" Josh waves a little, grinning wide. "I would hug you, but if he's right, that might not be what you want..."

"Hug?" Anton drags his eyes away from Cyrus and takes a good look at the stranger beside him. "I don't... I don't hug... anymore..."

"There a reason for that?"

Anton glances away, arm falling. "Y-yeah."

He turns and goes back into his room, leaving the door open as an invitation. With his back to the duo he shimmies a shirt on, ignoring how it clings to his damp skin.

"Sorry, no chairs... You're welcome to the bed though" He says, gesturing.

The two boys take the offered bed's edge and Josh casually puts an arm around Cyrus to pull him closer and make room for Anton on the bed too. He juts his head towards the spot so Anton knows he can sit. Anton does, but he is clearly uncomfortable with the proximity, sitting straight and stiff with his hands shoved against his legs.

"So uh... So you... Do we? Know each other?"

"I once moved into a new neighborhood... Met a really tall, really cute boy. I thought he'd be my first friend the second he told me his name... But, he ended up avoiding me. I can't say I blame him after what my parents did, but... Cyrus thinks it's you..."

Anton can't bring himself to look at Josh. The story sounds familiar, but wrong. Is it? Is he? There's no way... "W-what... what was his name?"

Josh leans down, kneels on the floor to force Anton to look at him. "Ant?" He whispers, addressing Anton directly.

He gasps, jerking backwards. "J-Joshie?"

The wide grin on Josh's face is wrong. It shouldn't be there. Anton shouldn't be here FUCK he has to leave. He has to get away, but Josh is in front of him. Maybe if he goes- No, Cyrus is there. Okay, okay it's fine. He can just... He can crawl backwards and- no, shit, the wall. Eyes darting rapidly, breath coming almost as quickly, Cyrus immediately recognizes that Anton is having a panic attack.

"Tony! Anton look at me! Look at me just like before okay? Breathe! Breathe in and then out... Everything is fine, we're all fine right? We're not moving, no touch okay? No touch. Just breathe with me alright big guy? Breathe... Good, good boy..."

Anton locks eyes with Cyrus and the world fades away.

He's right. They aren't moving. Moving is the problem. If he just sits still, he'll be okay. They'll all be okay. Breathing in with Cyrus feels right, yes. Okay he's breathing out. Yes, they're okay. They're gonna be okay.

Josh stands quietly and smiles softly. Neither has realized it, but Anton's pinky is touching Cyrus's leg, like he's subconsciously seeking comfort and touch from the other man. He decides to keep it to himself, so Anton doesn't panic again. But he can tell it's big.

When Anton calms down finally, Josh has already found some things to make tea in his room, and prepared some for the three of them. Holding the tiny edges, he hands the (plastic, he chuckles to himself noting) teacup to Anton.

"Here, some warm tea buddy. I've got... I've got something you should know, I think. And I... I want to apologize on behalf of my parents... I'm sure they meant well, for me, but they... Well lemme just..."

He sighs, sips his own tea, and starts again.

"I'm sorry, Ant-uh Anton. My parents told your mother that you hurt me when we met. It is true that my rib was fractured, and that when you hugged me, it caused a little pain. But... But the truth is, my rib was already fractured. You didn't do that. My... My parents just... Well they said you did, so that they could get out of paying the insurance company the ridiculous fees they wanted to charge us. So, if the fault was someone else, those fees would be lessened. Mostly because we wouldn't be paying."

Anton is frowning, frozen with the cup halfway to his mouth.

"But, if I didn't... I heard it, I heard the sound. It happened when I hugged you, I know it did!"

Josh shakes his head. "Nuh uh. A little while before we met, I fractured my rib in dance class. I'm a dancer, it's what I do and back then they tried to fit me with this masculine position. I was learning lifts, as in lifting other people. But" Josh pinches his lips together "But that was never my thing. I wasn't... Made for that, especially at that age. I was more fit for being lifted. So, the strain of the repetitive lifting, combined with my tiny frame, I just... yeah. Tiny little fracture. Your hug didn't do it."

Anton exhales shakily, mind reeling. That... was a lie? He didn't hurt Josh? He could have... He could have had a friend?

"But then... Your parents?"

"Like I said, they lied. In hindsight, I suppose I get it from their point of view, but it was still... a really shitty thing to do. I'd really like to apologize to your mother, as well, sometime. I know..."

He clears his throat and glances away tactfully. "I understand things were not... easy... back then. You know, for anyone..."

Quiet for a moment, Anton mulls over this new information. And then, "My mother? What... What do you mean things were hard?"

"Well..." Josh rubs the back of his neck, clearly uncomfortable, unsure of how to broach the topic as a whole. "I... I knew it was just you and your mom..." He starts, gauging Anton's reaction. Seeing just general confusion, he continues as gently as he can. "Your dad wasn't around, right?"

Anton shakes his head. "No, I made him go away... I broke him and my mom."

Cyrus speaks now, clearly startled. "What do you mean you broke them?"

He hangs his head, and shakes it again. "I'd... rather not please..."

"Right, no, sorry that's my fault" Cyrus corrects quickly, waving his hand where Anton can see it. "It's okay, I apologize. Go on Josh"

"Your mom, she worked a lot... From ah... from what I could tell. I mean, she must have, with all those payments she sent to my parents, plus whatever you guys had to live on, yeah? So I... You know, I just... It had to be hard. And, for whatever amount of that hardship was caused by my parents... I'm sorry. I'm really, really sorry."

"I dunno if it was any harder than most to be honest. I got an allowance, dunno how much it was compared to anyone else. Didn't really have friends to compare with. We got food, though I ate less than her so I could-"

He stops, clacks his teeth shut, as if realizing he's sharing too much. Would they judge him? He glances at Cyrus before blushing in embarrassment and looking away. He would... He wouldn't like the end of that sentence, probably...

"Well, yeah, so... I don't... I didn't ever think we were struggling? But, thank you, I suppose..."

"Ahhh let's not be sad. I finally get that friend I wanted all those years ago, this should be a celebration!! What do you say... Cyrus?"

Josh has a mischievous sparkle in his eyes with the way he says the honorific, and Cyrus has to tongue at his cheek to keep from saying anything. Anton has had enough cardiac stress for one morning. He does glance at him, though, while he isn't looking. He doesn't seem bothered by the term... Could it really have been him? Was he... Did he think of him that way? Did he imagine... No... No couldn't be...

"Coming with me?"

Heat flares up Cyrus's neck, his ears pinken, and he jolts on the bed. Anton's bed. The bed he-

"What? I'm-Um.... What?"

Anton seems oblivious to the state of his friend, as he repeats, "Josh said he was gonna tell your Professor that you're unwell, and he's taking you to the infirmary. I'm going to go pick up some food for us all. Are you coming with me, or...?"

"Right, right food yeah... Food... Let's get that." He stands up and eyes the bed sideways. Tries (and fails) to not imagine how Anton laid upon it while chanting his name. Moaning it, according to Josh... Fuck...

The trio moved to Cyrus's room, for plausible deniability according to Josh, while they ate their food. He'd waited for them at the corner of their hallway, linking his arm with Cyrus's when they returned. He chuckled to himself when he saw Anton blink at the gesture. Piling onto Cyrus's bed, Josh once again maneuvers himself to touch Cyrus as much as possible. It doesn't seem forced, though, as Anton watches. Based on Cyrus's response... or lack thereof really... This must be normal. Maybe Cyrus didn't mean anything before...

He watches Cyrus pick up his burger and lift it to his mouth as he recalls the elder's offer to hold hands. His own hands are tingling as he watches, itching for... something. He glances then, to Josh, who is carefully watching him watch Cyrus.

'Shit' he thinks, glancing down at his own untouched food.

"Say, Anton... It's a good thing your room is so close to Cyrus'."

"Is it?" Anton asks.

"Wha?" Cyrus says, simultaneously, with a mouth full of food.

"MM. It's great, really! I was hoping you could settle a little... dispute... Cyrusssss and I were having earlier."

Anton's brows are furrowed, imagining what kind of topic they could possibly be arguing about, let alone that he could settle just because he lives near to Cyrus. Maybe something about Cyrus's habits? Cyrus's eyes are wide, however, as he immediately senses where the topic is going. He elbows Josh who just howls in laughter and rushes to continue, crawling a little closer to Anton as he does. Not touching, but closer to him and further from Cyrus's elbow.

"So, I was walking down the plaza the other day and mentioned to Cyrus I'd heard something strange. He says he didn't hear or do anything. Maybe you could help?"

"Strange? I haven't... heard anything strange... when was it? Was it loud?"

Josh giggles throatily. "Oh it was loud"

"Josh Daniels stop do not ask him!"

"Oh come onnn bro. If you insist you weren't up to anything, then maybe Anton knows something!"

"Josh you know why."

"Do I?" He smiles and shrugs, feigning innocence.

"I'm confused... Am I... supposed to know something Cyrus was doing? Or... Because I assure you my room is entirely too far away for me to hear what he's doing in his own... I mean, I didn't even know about the guitar until I visited here..."

"Oh, so you visit do you? You visit often?"

"N-no? Just the once... twice now, if you include this one..."

"Mmm. And did you visit the other day?"

"Yes?" Anton asks, looking between Cyrus and Josh for the correct answer.

Josh sits on his feet, a little closer to Anton than before, and smiles. "So, you wouldn't happen to have heard, or seeeeen, if someone came into his room that same day hmm?"

"I- Um... No? No I wouldn't, why?"

Leaning back dramatically, Josh dips his head back to gaze at Cyrus from his lap, the latter holding his food up and away so it doesn't get all over him, and sighs.

"WELLL I was walking down the plaza the other day, and I could have sworn Cyrus had some *ahem* company over, because I heard them chanting his name in the most beauuutiful prayer."

"Cyrus- please Cyyyy" He whines, gasping for air between each word and moaning on the end of the phrase.

Above him, Cyrus averts his gaze, desperately trying to hide his own flush and avoid looking at Anton. Fuck why was Josh like this. Anton must be so embarrassed. Wait, what if it wasn't him? What if someone else-

He looks up and meets Anton's startled gaze. It feels like the first time they're really seeing each other and Cyrus wishes he could lurch forward and capture Anton's lips in his own because... fuck... fuck he is pretty... Instead, he locks his knees where they are, grips his burger so hard the toppings fall out, and waits... Waits for Anton's denial to fall out of his lips. Waits so he can figure out some kind of joke to laugh it off and make him feel better...

Anton inhales, then exhales, then inhales again... When he speaks it's a whisper, and his eyes are still locked with Cyrus's.

"Y-you heard that...?"

It's a question, aimed at Cyrus, and Cyrus isn't sure what he wants him to say. Does he lie and say yes? Is he hoping he did? Would that make it worse?

"N-no... He did, I... I didn't..."

Anton's exhale looks like relief, and Cyrus's belly clenches. He's relieved, okay... Good answer Cy, good answer.

"Do you... Like me?"

Josh and Cyrus both jolt upright and stare at Anton. He's looking at his hands, voice loud in the room but still gentle somehow.

"Hmmm?" He adds, eyes flicking up to Cyrus's hands again. "I... If I'm wrong, I apologize. But, I... I want to be honest with you. It was... It was me. I was... Was..."

He swallows, and Cyrus notices then that he looks like he's shivering. He instinctively reaches a hand out, stopping a few inches away as he realizes what he's doing.

"No touch, right. I'm sorry. It's... habit."

Anton chuckles and gestures at Josh, who just grins. "I can tell."

"If I say I do, does that... Is that what you want to hear?"

"Only if it's the truth... Because... I think I like you, too. And I...
I want..."

Anton raises his hand, inches it closer to Cyrus's as it hovers
near him. "I want to... you know... I just..."

As his hand falls away, Cyrus releases the breath he didn't
know he was holding. Beside him, Josh does the same.

"Um, I'd like to use the restroom, if you don't mind... s'cuse
me... be back in a minute" he says, excusing himself with a
'thumbs up' at the door aimed at Cyrus.

The silence as Josh leaves is full, ripe for picking, and Cyrus
can't take it anymore. He scoots a little closer, knees almost
touching Anton's, and leans his head down to catch his gaze.

"You want to touch, don't you?"

Anton refuses to look at him, just nods. He nods like he's
ashamed to want to touch, and it breaks Cyrus's heart a little
more.

"Can you look at me?... Please Tony?"

He shakes his head, hair flopping rapidly.

"Do you... Why does it seem like you are ashamed to want to
touch? To want to be touched? Do you know?"

He glances up then, lips pursed. "Because I should be. I should
be ashamed. I shouldn't want that b-because... I don't... deserve
it... I hurt people remember?"

"Tony... listen to me. Josh told you already, you didn't hurt him
right? What if... What if there are more stories like that? What if

there were misunderstandings, or things just beyond your control? Huh? Will you... Can we look into it, together?"

"That wouldn't..." Anton sighs heavily. "It's more than that. A misunderstanding wouldn't explain broken teapots, or dead fish, or-or my mom in th-the hospital"

He chokes on the end of the sentence, gaze averted again. He doesn't want to see Cyrus's look change... the way he sees him... He wants to remember the pretty eyes on him like he... like he mattered. Like he was normal.

Cyrus sighs and leans back. "Anton... I really want you to look at me... please... It's taking everything in me not to kiss you, and I'm running out of the self-restraint I need to keep from doing that... or turning your face to me..."

Anton can't help but jerk his gaze upwards, choking once again on air.

"Y-you want to..." He swallows, whispering "K-kiss m-me? But... Even though...?"

"Yes, you big beautiful man. I want to kiss you, and I want to hold your hand, and I want you to wrap your stupidly big arms around me so I can feel safe and protected and... and FUCK I wanna do the same to you too you know? I just... Fuck..."

He sighs and runs a hand through his hair.

"I want to do a lot of things, Anton, but all of them involve touch. But you know what I want to do so much more than I want to touch you?"

"Mm?" Anton blinks at him, eyes shining with the birth of tears.

"I want to love you. I want to protect you. I want to take you to a nice restaurant for dinner, and buy you flowers, and lay down on my bed at night talking to you on the phone or something... I don't need to touch you. I'm..." He looks up at Anton again, taking a deep breath as he continues. "I'm prepared to never touch you for the rest of our lives if it means I could have a shot at loving you. That's what I want, Anton. So yeah, I guess you could say I like you..."

"I can't... I can't. I can admit I want to, Cy, but I can't... touch..."

"I know. I know Tony, it's okay. I'm going to work very hard on respecting that for you, okay? I promise you."

Anton nods sheepishly. "I like you too."

Cyrus snorts now, leaning back and picking at what remains of the innards of his burger. "I... guessed as much... considering, you know..." He waves at the door, indicating Josh's former presence.

"Yeah... about that... I'm sorry. I didn't mean for... Well anyone... to hear me..."

"It's 'kay. Maybe you can tell me about it sometime, hm?"

He laughs then, at Anton's incredulous expression, assuring him he was only kidding. "Unless...?"

Date night, the next weekend

Cyrus stands outside Anton's dorm, just around the corner, trying to swallow the massive lump in his throat. Getting ready for a date you actually care about, in a dorm shower with a half dozen other dudes, is no easy feat. But, here he is. Long hair mousse'd into gentle curls, a suit jacket layered over a simple white v-neck and his nicest pair of light-washed blue-jeans. He absolutely looks like a college student going on a date, but whatever. It's probably fine.

In his hands he carefully holds the plant life for his date, praying he made the right choice in straying away from traditional flowers. He wanted something for Tony that would last longer. Something to prove he's not the actual God of Destruction. So what did he buy? A teeny little baby miniature tree. He wasn't entirely sure what the species was, maybe plum? The lady at the store had passed this one to him when he asked for something that would, eventually, bloom. He hoped Tony would enjoy that little surprise whenever it came. With a deep breath, Cyrus fills his lungs and pulls his shoulders back. He couldn't keep his big man waiting, not if he wanted to maximize the amount of time he could, within socially acceptable parameters, stare at his stupid face.

He almost hides the plant behind his back, but then he recalls Anton's concern about clumsiness being "contagious" around him while they texted each other. He laughs, but opts to still hold the plant in front of him, and off to the side, hidden by the edge of the doorway.

Knock knock

He swallows the nerves sucking the moisture out of his mouth and waits, hoping like hell his sweaty palms don't drop anything. He needs this to go well. Super well. The wellest. Because he has to prove to Anton he's not a curse. He's a really good man, and he deserves love.

There's a thud followed by a crash, and the distinct sound of tumbling items and a mumbling Anton, before the door opens with a yank. And there, disheveled and clearly nursing a bleeding toe, stands Cyrus's date for the night. He's in a sweater, his hair has fallen all over his face, still damp, his own jeans match the colour of Cyrus's, and he's still barefoot.

"Shit... I'm sorry I'm late I'm so late... Come in?" He says, turning to look once more for his other shoe.

Cyrus hides his laugh behind a cough, pretending not to watch as Anton bends down onto his hands and knees, head to the floor, looking under his bed. His breath hitches as Anton reaches for something, his sweater exposing a sliver of skin at his back. 'What, am I fucking 15 again? It's just some skin man get a grip' he berates himself silently, closing his eyes tightly. When he opens them again, Anton is sitting up, face bright red and flushed, damp hair framing his stupidly cute face... and Cyrus groans.

"Ah, sorry, really!"

"No no, it's not you babe. It's me. It's 100% me"

"Ba- ah... right... um... right. Shoes."

Cyrus winces and shouts, "Wait!"

When Anton flinches, he realizes how loud he shouted. "I mean, hang on Tony, you should put a bandage on that... So you don't ruin your socks, you know?"

Anton blinks and looks down at his bleeding toe. "Right... Yeah that's... I don't have any?"

Cyrus smiles softly, squatting down next to Anton. "Silly Tony. Here, this is for you. It um... It's not flowers, right now, but... eventually it will be."

He gently sets the bonsai next to him and dashes out of the room to his own for a bandage. When he returns, Anton is in exactly the same place he left him, holding the tree like it's made of glass.

"Do you... like it?"

"I love it" Anton says, breathlessly "No one's... This is so thoughtful, I... I didn't get you anything"

The fact that he pouts as he says that, sends Cyrus's heart fluttering. This man might actually be the death of him at this rate. He doesn't realize he's just staring, until Anton clears his throat.

"Ah, sorry, just... You look really cute... Here you go" He looks away, holding out the bandage.

"Thanks" Anton says, not sure which he's really thanking him for.

Once Anton has patched himself up and slipped his shoes on, Cyrus holds open his dorm door for him like a gentleman. And every subsequent door, actually. Anton isn't sure if he's doing it to keep Anton from hurting them both, or if it's just how dates work but... it's cute. Cyrus scoots his chair in for him, too. Pours the wine for him. Anton never really notices when he's low on water, because Cyrus pours that too. It's like he's just... in tune with whatever Anton is in need of, before Anton realizes, and takes care of it.

And that's exactly how Anton feels. Taken care of.

Especially as they walk along the river after their meal. It's a comfortable silence, with Cyrus standing apart but close enough it's obvious they're walking together. As his gaze falls on the smaller man beside him, Anton becomes aware. More aware than he thinks he's ever been in his life, really. Because he's watching this man walking beside him, with no fear, gazing out at the river like it doesn't matter that he's walking beside Anton. He's not afraid of him. It hits him, then, too.

He's not afraid either. He's walked for at least 20 minutes and hasn't once had an intrusive thought about whether Cyrus would die of drowning because Anton tripped, landed on him, and threw him into the river. He didn't fret about Cyrus choking at dinner, or knocking the candle over and setting the restaurant on fire, or even whether the bus they rode on would crash and burn. Even now, as he thinks about those scenarios, he isn't afraid of them.

They could still happen, he knows. But he hears Cyrus's voice in his head.

"If I avoided everything that could hurt me, I would be living in a bubble that doesn't exist."

Anton glances down at Cyrus's hands as they sway gently. Holding hands could hurt them. A lot could go wrong. Cyrus could fall in the river after all. He could get crushed beneath Anton if they tripped over each other. Again. Anton wasn't sure he was ready for that.

But still...

"Cy?" he asks, stopping his steps.

Cyrus turns and stops beside him, immediately, and hums in response. "Hmm?"

"If I touch you, you could get hurt... right? Be... be honest..."

The elder tilts his head and is quiet for a moment, before nodding. "Yes, I suppose there is a timeline where I could be hurt if you touched me. Why do you ask?"

Anton is breathing heavy, but steady, like he's gasping in air and forcing it out of his body, bracing himself for something. Like the first time a kid goes to jump off the deep end of a full sized swimming pool.

"I... I don't think... I don't think I'm ready for that."

Cyrus nods immediately this time, fluffy hair bouncing across his pinkened cheeks. "That's fine, I told you-"

"So can you... Can you..." Anton's breaths come a little faster now, shoulders pushed back, gaze boring into Cyrus's. "Can you put your hands on me? Instead? L-like before?"

Eyebrows disappear into Cyrus's hairline as his jaw drops open. "Wha-You don't have to do that Tony, I really am okay with however you want us..."

Anton nods rapidly. "I know. That's just it I... I want..." His eyes well up with tears as he pushes through the emotions he's feeling. Fear, excitement, anxiety and... Something else?

"Take your time big guy, it's okay. What do you want? Do you want me to touch you?"

Anton Shakes his head now. "No I..."

"No? Then I won't, it's easy."

"No, It, that's..... I..... What I want is to touch you. I want... I wanted to hold your hand on this walk b-but... It's too much. I... I can't. But if you..."

Cyrus chuckles then, shoulders relaxing. "If I touch you and not the other way around, that feels like beating the system, right?"

"Y-yeah... kinda... Is that weird? That's weird isn't it..."

"Not at all" Cyrus replies, stepping a little closer and tilting his head to look Anton in his eyes. How he wishes he could stroke those tears away for him.

"Are you sure you want me to touch you?"

Anton nods, chewing on a lip. "P-please..."

They both swallow, hard, as Cyrus lifts his hand up... up... up... and hovers it over Anton's chest. He looks up for one more confirmation before carefully easing it onto his body. The younger's lips part in a soft gasp and the world fades away from both of them. This moment is so huge that it's wrapped them both in a bubble. How long have they stood here? How many tears have streamed down Anton's cheeks? Why are Cyrus's wet as well?

"Wow..." Anton finally manages, breathless.

"Yeah... wow..." Cyrus says, equally affected. How magical something as simple as touch can be. Cyrus wonders, then, how Anton has managed to live without this very thing for so long. It's so simple, so necessary, and yet...

Cyrus swears to himself, then, that so long as Anton lets him he will make up for those years without touch. He doesn't care if he's in the middle of a work day, if Anton asks for his touch he will drop everything to give it. Anton's hand comes up, shaking, and hovers near Cyrus's. He wants to return the favour, so badly but what if...

"Anton LOOK OUT"

His head whips around as he grabs at Cyrus and throws him to the grass, squeezing his eyes shut as the speeding moped crashes directly into his side. He barely registers the colour of the thing as his body erupts in pain. Cyrus cries out, half in pain and half in shock, as Anton is struck. As soon as Anton hits the sidewalk, Cyrus is crawling over to him, wincing as his own wrist throbs in pain.

"Tony? TONY are you okay? Tony please"

     Anton had managed to bring an arm up to cushion his head from the concrete, but his arm was now bent at an unsettling angle, and purple was already settling around the area. He blinks his eyes open, winces, and looks quickly at Cyrus.

"Cyrus are you okay? Are you... I touched you did you... Please be okay Cy please"

     They're both crying again, still in their bubble as the driver of the moped lifts his helmet off and paces, calling for an ambulance.

     "Silly Tony I'm fine, you gotta lay still though okay? Don't *sniff* don't move okay? Can... can I wipe your face?...Please?"

Anton nods numbly, head throbbing a little. "Y-yeah I think... if you're really okay... if I didn't... yeah... you're okay right?"

     Cyrus nods, tears on his own face, as he wraps his good hand in a sweater paw and wipes the streaks on Anton's. "I'm alright, you saved me Anton it's okay... I'm okay, and you're gonna be okay yeah?"

"I... saved you?"

"Yes you big oak, you saved me."

Anton giggles a little. "Hnn... Called me an Oak"

"Well you are, aren't you? Great big thing and for what? Protecting us little guys right?"

"Mm. Maybe shade in the summer?"

"Exactly. You're gonna be my shade and I'm gonna carve my initials in you."

'You already have' Anton thinks, unable to voice the words as the paramedics arrive and nudge Cyrus aside to get him loaded first. He's surprised, at first, when they let Cyrus ride in the back as well, until he notices one of them tending to his arm.

"Cy what-"

"It's fine Anton, just a sprain probably. Right?" He nudges the person wrapping his arm, who nods quickly. "See? I'm okay, basically the same injury I did to myself just the other day."

Anton's brows furrow, thinking how Cyrus wouldn't have that injury if he hadn't pushed him. As the paramedic tending to him adjusts his arm, however, that thought is thrown out the window. Because if he hadn't pushed him, would Cyrus be here, now? In this pain?

No. He made the right choice. Better him than Cyrus, Cyrus didn't deserve to be hurt. He deserved to be protected, and safe. Anton could do that... Right?

☞ ☜

They're separated, once they arrive at the hospital, to be treated simultaneously. Cyrus is done faster, however, after an x-ray cleared him of any breaks. Just a sprain confirmation and given basic care instructions. When he's finally allowed to visit Anton's room, he puts what he hopes is a calm face on and pushes the door open. Anton's eyes are blown wide, clearly on pain killers if the dopey little smile on his face is anything to go by.

"So what'd they say big guy? You getting a bionic arm or something?"

"Hehe Cyyyyyyruuuuuus."

"Yeah it's me Tony" Cyrus says softly, approaching the bedside.

"Hi" Anton replies just as softly, dimple creasing his face as he smiles.

"You're feeling pretty good right now, aren't you?"

"Always good... when you're 'round."

Cyrus snorts, "Ah, is that so? How good?"

"Reeeeeal gooood. Good when you're not, too."

"Oh really?"

"Mmm."

"How is it good when I'm not around?"

"Because even when you're not, you are, you know? You're always 'round. Always round and round and round." Anton giggles then and Cyrus's heart staccatos in his chest.

"Shhh sh that's enough from you mister. You're gonna say something you regret..."

"Nahhhhh no regrets. No bubbles. Right Cy? No bubbles. That's life"

"Sure Anton, that's life. You okay? Your arm?"

"Ohhhh.YeahhhIam.Said'sbroke.Someotherwordsbut they said not bad? Just broke. Heyy you have one too!"

Anton holds his bound arm up beside Cyrus's braced one and grins again. "Yours is a baby cast though. Baby cast for baby Cyyyy"

"Oh I'm the baby huh?"

Anton pouts. He's the baby? That's... No, not him. Tony is the baby, that's why Cy is Cy.

Cyrus tries very hard not to laugh as Anton whisper-converses with himself. He probably doesn't even realize he's doing it.

He texts Josh as quickly as he can, arm considering, and barely manages to finish the first text before his phone starts ringing, loudly.

Anton immediately starts mimicking the sound, causing Cyrus to answer the phone with a delirious little chuckle.

"H-hello Josh?"

"Are- what the fuck is happening in the background where are you ARE YOU OKAY WHAT THE FUCK HAPPENED-"

"Shhhh sh sh stop yelling I'm FINE okay? And if you can't tell by the giggling in the back, Anton is more than fine. They've given him some pain killers, and it looks like he broke his arm. But he's fine"

"BROKE HIS- That's it I'm coming down there which hospital is it? Text me the address right now bye"

Cyrus sighs and tugs a chair closer to Anton's bed. They settle in a comfortable silence, the only sound the *tap tap tap* of

Cyrus's fingers on his phone as he sends out the hospital's address and room number to Josh.

When he looks up, Anton is quietly staring at him, grinning with half-visible eyes until he notices Cyrus looking back at him.

"Hi" he whispers.

"Hi yourself handsome"

gasp "You think I'm handsome?"

"Very, actually. Does that bother you?"

"Nahhh. I think you're handsome too. I like you a lot."

Cyrus blushes and rests his head on his good hand. "You shouldn't say things like that right now Anton. I might... Might believe you, you know? And you might not be ready for me to know them yet."

"Naaaaaahs'okay.Ithinkallthetime.Thinkthinkthink.S'better to talk sometimes right?"

"Sometimes, sure..." Cyrus concedes before adding, "But, I think it's better to only talk when you are fully in control of yourself. Which you aren't right now, are you?"

Anton grins and rolls his head back to stare at the ceiling. "Mmm... Prolly not"

"There you go. So whatever you have said so far, let's pretend I didn't hear it okay?"

"Sure, sure. But if I say it later does that mean we don't have to pretend anymore?"

"That's fine, if you say it, say, tomorrow. Deal?"

"Deal. Shake on it?" Anton asks.

Cyrus jerks a little, surprised. "Sh-shake on it? That means touching Anton, I'm not touching you until tomorrow at least... You can't... You can't consent to- Wait, why are you laughing?"

Anton's giggles spill over as he gently shakes his cast. "Hehe get it Hyung? Shake on it? We can shake our broken bits heheh"

Cyrus sighs and shakes his brace at Anton. "Okay, we shook on it. Good?"

"Hehe yeah, good. We made a chicken deal. That's serious, you know."

"Riiight right. Chicken deal."

"Yeahhh. I like chicken. You like chicken?"

"I do... Our next date we'll get some chicken yeah?"

Anton gasps, eyes wide. "You want another date? Oh my god was I bad on this one?"

Cyrus giggles. "No silly, you were perfect. That's why I want another one."

"Ahhh okay. My first date, I did okay. Good good." Anton is gettingsleepy,now,lidsdrooping,andCyrusstartstowhisperto coax him the rest of the way.

"My perfect little oak date" He uses the nurse's pen to move Anton's hair away from his face before sitting down in the chair again and curling up to nap.

"Oak... Saved Cyrus. Good boy Ant... did good..." Anton
mutters as he drifts away.

When Josh arrives at the hospital, he's glad he stops at the
nurse's station to ask for directions, because they tell him the two
occupants have been napping. So, he doesn't barge in with a
scream like he'd originally intended. He even brought a friend to
dramatically hold him back.

That friend hovers near the door, unsure if he should enter
considering he doesn't know the man actually in the bed. All Josh
had told him was it was Cyrus's boyfriend. But he didn't even
know Cyrus had a boyfriend. Josh steps towards the two sleeping
figures, and smiles. They fell asleep with faces turned to each
other, like they were talking as they drifted.

'Cute' he thinks.

He turns and steps closer to his friend, whispering, "It's okay,
just don't touch the one in the bed. He doesn't do touch."

"Germaphobe?" he whispers back.

Josh shakes his head with a grim smile "No, it's... a past thing.
You remember that kid I mentioned, that my parents took
advantage of his mom?"

"Ohhh Ant right? Is that him?"

Nodding, Josh's smile gets tighter. "Yeah. He thought he
actually broke my ribs... It's a long story, we'll have to tell you
later, but-"

Anton's voice croaks from the bed, breaking their whispered
conversation with a "MeMe?"

Jamie freezes, eyes wide. "Y-yes?"

Josh is frowning, looking between them in confusion. "Do you already know each other?"

"I... don't think so? I don't know an Ant"

"...oh" Anton says, shoulders slumping a little. "Right. Y-yeah, makes sense... Sorry, I-I must be mistaken..."

Jamie steps a little closer, brows furrowed. "No, you... You said my name, but I haven't... used that..."

He leans over the bed, trying to see Anton's face clearly, but the latter keeps his head turned away to hide the way his vision blurs once more.

"Josh said I can't touch you... so... Can you turn and face me please?I-Yousaidmyname,wemustknoweachother,right?"

Anton turns, but keeps his gaze trained to the cast on his arm. "N-Not if you don't want us to."

"Wait" Josh says, approaching the other side of the bed. "Anton... You do know him right? You recognize him? From where?"

"S-same as you..."

There's silence for a moment and it's the uncomfortable kind that Anton doesn't know what to do with. He'd normally leave the area, but he's not only ill-equipped for that, he's also trapped with the two men on either side of his bed.

He keeps his eyes trained down, not wanting to make anyone else more uncomfortable than they already must be.

"I'm sorry... I'm sorry if I... Mm... Make you uncomfortable... I ah... If you want me to go, I c-can. You're here for Cyrus I assume so... So I can..."

"Heyy what are you saying? We're here for both of you Anton. And this is your hospital room!"

"S'okay I... I can still..." Anton's cheeks are hot, slowly shining wet in the dim lighting.

"Shhh sh sh no Anton, look at me. Can you do that?" Josh says, leaning down as close as he dares.

When Anton finally looks, briefly, at his face, it lights up in a bright sunshine smile, full of teeth and crinkles around his eyes.

"There we go. We just want you to tell us the truth, okay? Not what you think we want to hear. Remember how you and I had different recollections of the same moment? We-" He looks up at Jamie and then back to Anton "We just want to make sure this isn't the same. So, from the beginning, how do you know Jamie? From childhood? Were you neighbors as well?"

Anton turns back to Jamie and looks up at him, finally. Seconds after he does, he gasps.

"Holy... you broke my nose!!"

Anton winces and leans away again immediately, mumbling apologies. Of course, of course he hurt him. He remembers the hurt, but not meeting him. He's forgettable without the injuries, because he's-

"That was the most hilarious moment of my childhood, one of my top five memories! I can't... I can't believe it's you!!"

"You... like that memory?" Anton asks, incredulously.

"Are you kidding me?? My parents gave me everything I wanted for the whole year after that incident!! Josh you remember that year, right? That's the year we met!!! I bribed you into friendship with-"

"-With a literal armload of candy yes oh my GOD you're telling me that was all because of Tony??"

"Yes!! Yes oh my god your name is Tony? Anton? Oh my god..."

"I hurt you... but you're happy?"

Jamie waves a hand dismissively, no longer bothering to try and be quiet at this point. "That was nothing, honestly I don't even think you actually broke broke my nose. Probably just made it bleed a little, but you bet I ran home and dramatically told my parents!! Besides, accidents happen. Sure, you were the one standing up, but I also was bending over. Honestly most of the kinetic energy was probably down to the force and speed of me bendinganyway.Howhardcouldyoustandup?Enoughtodo that? Nahhh"

"Wait... So did I hurt you, and you're happy? Or did I not..." Anton is confused, head pounding almost as loudly as his arm is throbbing. He winces and holds it closer to him instinctively.

Josh notices and gently pushes the call button for a nurse.

"Okay big guy, let's get you some pain meds, and let you rest, yeah?"

"No no no I can't take them! Not yet" Anton leans back, but looks over at Cyrus's sleeping form. "I can't yet. Not today."

"Why... not today? You just broke your arm, today is definitely the day of all days you should take some relief."

Anton shakes his aching head violently back and forth. "No. I can't. Cyrus said... He said I can't say what I said unless I was in control of my own mind. We have to pretend he didn't hear it until then. I don't... I don't want to pretend. I want him to know."

Josh's eyes close slowly, biting back a grin that fights to escape.

"I see. Well, in that case, Jamie how about you and I go see what Anton here needs to be discharged, yeah?"

The nurse arrives at the door just as they leave it. Josh tells her he was simply letting her know that Anton is awake, and they are ready to get the discharge process going. She nods and turns, taking them to the main desk.

"So you know Jamie already huh?"

Anton blinks over at Cyrus, eyes wide, as the elder speaks without moving or even opening his eyes.

"Y-you're awake?"

He gets a grunt in response.

"...oh"

"Mm."

"Y-yeah, um... Dunno if I mentioned it but... There was a kid... I knew him as MeMe... Or, rather, he introduced himself as Meme..." Anton swallows and continues softly. "When he introduced himself, I was alone... by a tree..."

Cyrus's eyes are open now, sweetly watching Anton tell his story. Full of patience. Anton likes that about Cyrus. There's never any pressure, never any rush. It makes him feel so safe.

"So um... when we met it was... kind of a disaster. I accidentally sent my book flying into his face, split his lip... And then when I went to stand up, to bow and apologize, I- Well, I stood up and his whole face was covered in blood. He ran away, and..." Anton sighs. "And I can't blame him. I went back to being alone like always. Safer that way."

Cyrus sits up slowly, scoots the chair right up against the bed, then lays his head on the edge of it. He doesn't say anything, just stays there, resting as near to Anton as he can. As close to holding him as he can be. So it's a shock, when he feels fingers in his hair. He freezes, not wanting to startle Anton.

"What...?"

"Been wanting to do this for a while... It's..."

"Mm?" Cyrus asks, tilting his head into the fingers a little, silently asking for more pressure.

Anton gives it, scratching his nails a little on his scalp, causing Cyrus to moan involuntarily.

"Fuck..."

"S'not my fault... feels good..."

"Yeah?" Anton chuckles softly "You'll have to show me sometime"

He does sit up then, fingers falling out of his hair. "You-"

Anton inhales, bracing himself, exhaling loudly. "I like you, Cy. I like you, I want to touch you, and I... I want you to touch me. I more than want it, I think. I just... Can we... Can we go slow? And um..."

Cyrus reaches his own good hand out, pinky touching Anton's carefully. A gentle offer. Anton loops their pinkies around each other as he continues, a broad smile painting his face.

"I need to go slow. Just... Just us, for now. Maybe soon... I hope soon... I just..."

"Shhh it's okay. I understand. I'll be your guinea pig" he winks at Anton, who scoffs in retort.

"Hey! That's not-"

They devolve into giggles, fingers lacing together slowly. One finger, two fingers, three. By the time the other two boys return with a doctor and a stack of paperwork, they have palms pressed and fingers locked together.

Josh and Jamie exchange knowing smiles.

Anton's room, later that night

Their shoes are kicked off into a massive pile just inside Anton's room the very second they land there. Josh takes one look at the place and tuts.

"Well this just is not going to work for me."

"What do you mean? Should we... Should we go to Cyrus's room instead?" Anton starts worrying immediately, until Josh smiles at him.

"Not at all Tony. I mean, with your arm entirely out of commission, this place needs a little... altering. So you can do everything one handed."

Anton blushes then, sitting carefully on the far side of his own bed, so he doesn't touch anyone. And, of course, so he's out of Josh's way... Who he quickly finds out is like a tornado of joy when he's let loose with cleaning products.

He's also pretty sure the man carries some in his bag, because he does not remember owning window cleaner, let alone one that smells like apples?

Jamie and Cyrus spend most of the time curled up on the bed talking with each other, as they seem completely used to Josh's cleaning mode. Cyrus does reach over and lace his fingers with Anton's and squeezes, letting him know he's there. It makes Anton feel... so many things. He knows, from watching the others interact with each other, that this little gesture is... honestly so very small. Strangers shake hands, even hug, so it should be so easy and so silly to feel the way he does about it.

He's not even sure if it's like this because it's been so long, or if it's like this because it's Cyrus. All he knows, is he wishes he could glue Cyrus's hands onto his body to stay there forever. Every touch sends a warm pulse that is not his own, rocketing down his veins. He can feel Cyrus's heartbeat through his fingers, in tiny little jumps against his hand. It makes his own hand tingle, like it's fallen asleep, but he feel like it's more alive than ever. He closes his eyes and leans back against the wall, relishing in the warmth of Cyrus's hand wrapped in his own. He surreptitiously rubs his thumb against it, feeling the ridges and bumps beneath it. He dopily opens one eye when Cyrus squeezes his hand in response.

The elder is looking at him with a soft smile, lips tight and curled upwards. His eyes squint a little like a cat looking at its owner, before he turns his attention back to Jamie. When Tornado-Josh is finally done, an hour or two later, he drops dramatically onto the bed, limbs strewn across the other two. He's busy showing his pruny fingers to Jamie, who cradles them in his own hands, kissing each one to "fluff it up". Anton has to smile at the incredulity of it, but it's sweet. He reminds himself that they're just friends, and they're freely touching, kissing, holding each other in ways he'd only ever dreamed of. They don't just tell each other they care, they show it.

They wrap each other up in their love like warm blankets and tender touches and it's... So much to take in, even from here. He feels something like jealously stir in his belly, and frowns. Is it jealousy? No... Maybe envy is better.

Cyrus scoots closer to him and flicks a finger against his nose softly.

"Hey"

"Mm? Oh, hi." Anton smiles, dimple creasing prettily. "Just thinking."

"I noticed. You were looking pretty hard at them. Something on your mind about them specifically, or is that just where your eyes were?"

"Ah... little of both?"

Cyrus nods and looks down at Anton's shoulder, wanting to lay his head on it, but unsure if that's too much, too soon. He settles for laying his head on the wall near it, tilting towards their twined hands.

"How lucky we are," He chuckles "That our injured arms are on the opposite sides."

Anton gasps and smiles broadly back at him. "How lucky indeed!"

His eyes drop to Cyrus's lips, wet as he flicks his tongue across them. His heart skips several beats as he imagines those lips on his own. He wonders if they're as soft as his hair was, or as warm as his fingers.

"Penny for your thoughts, Tony" those lips whisper. Anton shivers as they pucker to say his name.

"Mm... wan' kiss you" he whispers back.

"Want... but can't yet... right?"

Anton swallows and tries to look away, nodding, but his chin is turned back with a single long finger from Cyrus.

"Ah ah, no more running right? No more bubble. We can go slow, okay? There's no pace but our pace, and my pace is yours."

"But... But what if you change your mind? What if it takes too long? What if you... what if you want to touch more, like they do?" He jerks his head to the other two, who are desperately pretending not to be paying attention to the couple.

"Tony. My sweet oak. I was prepared to spend the rest of my life, as long as you would have me, with absolutely no touch at all. I would be content with that. This?" He holds up their joined hands "This is... incredible. You make this incredible for me. I wouldn't dream of having anyone else."

There is dramatic retching from beside them, Jamie and Josh feigning having to throw up as they smile at them.

"DIS GUS TIN' the both of you! I'm out! TonTon, good luck
with... all of him... and remember that things are changed in here
okay?"

"Yes! Ooh and if you need anything, here's my number. I'm
really really happy we can be friends now, To-Anton. Really."
Jamie drops a paper with beautiful handwriting and a phone
number on it, onto the bed where Anton can reach it.

   And then, they're alone. The silence that should be, would be
suffocating with anyone else, is simply comfortable. The *tick tick
tick* of the built-in clock on the wall is the only sound besides the
blood rushing in their ears, and it's nice.

   Cyrus breaks the silence for once. He inhales through his nose,
exhaling through the same quickly. "So..."

"Mm?"

His throat bobs, catching Anton's gaze, before he speaks
again.

"You um... Could you maybe tell me about that time? What..."
His eyes are dark, lidded, wanting, as he looks up into Anton's
again. "What did you want me to do to you?"

Anton's breath hitches immediately and his hand squeezes
Cyrus's tightly.

"...Fuck" he whispers.

   "Well, we could but that requires touching so... How 'bout you
just tell me about it? Or... Or would you rather watch?"

   Anton's chest is heaving as he tries to figure out what oxygen is
again. "I-what-you-fuck.... fuck......"

Cyrus giggles and bites his lip. "It's your choice... baby..."

"Cyyyyyrusss you can't just... come on..."

He whines a little when Cyrus pulls his hand away, freezing when he realizes why he did. Cyrus has drifted his hand over to his own body, and is trailing his fingertips up and down his own chest.

"Tell me, Tony. Tell me what you want to see. What do you want your eyes to touch? We can start there." When Anton hesitates, he briefly tugs his shirt up and then his waistband down, exposing a sliver of pale skin.

He looks to Anton, who is wide-eyed and entranced following Cyrus's motions.

"Tell me... Tell me what you want, don't be afraid. Whatever it is... I wanna do it okay?"

Anton's eyes flit back to his own, pupils swallowing the hooded orbs. "W-what... What do you want? Don't... Don't just say what I want, I wanna know... I wanna know what you want too..."

"You want me to be honest?" Anton grunts affirmative, eyes locking on Cyrus's lips as he speaks. "Okay baby. I waaant... I wanna to hear your voice. Wanna watch you watch me, while I touch myself. While I touch where you want me to touch. Want... Wanna watch you touch yourself, Anton. Fuck, I wanna hear your sweet little sounds... Josh said you were begging, that day... were you?"

Anton nods, cheeks flaming. "Y-yeah..."

"Say it... please say it, whatever you said that day. Please let me hear it?"

"I was…"

"Go on"

"I was begging, Cy…"

"Begging for what?"

Cyrus palms himself through his pants with his good hand, listening intently. Anton's eyes are trained on the motions as he breathes heavily trying to speak.

"Begging for… for you. For you to touch me… t-to…"

"Yes?"

"For you to l-love me… to hold me like a l-lover…"

"I do" Cyrus replies immediately "Fuck, I do. I will. I promise I will love you like that someday Tony."

"Yeah? Can you um…"

"Anything, name it"

"Call me cute?"

Cyrus halts his motions, straining to sit up a little higher, a little closer to Anton's face. "You, my beautiful little Oak tree, are exceptionally cute."

"Yeah?"

"Fuck yes."

"P-promise?"

"I promise you, there is not a cuter boy in this entire school."

"...There's you"

Cyrus blushes and snorts a little, the two of them laughing tenderly. "Okay, maybe we tie then."

He looks back up into Anton's eyes, taking in his face... the way his lips are pink and bitten, begging to be caressed.

"Wanna kiss you, Tony. Wanna feel your lips between mine."

"Mm... me too..."

"Wanna taste every fucking inch of you... Bet you taste so sweet..."

"Mm... Cy?"

"Yeah?"

"Can we... I'm so hard..."

"Shit, Tony, you and me both"

Cyrus drops his head against the wall, hard, and groans. The tent in his pants is evident now that Anton looks at it, and he can't help the soft puff of air that escapes his mouth.

"Wanna see you. Can we touch ourselves?...Please?"

"Are you sure? We don't... We don't have to."

"Want to. Need to. Wanna watch you too"

"Fuck. Okay. Yeah. Yeah, let's..."

"Just... the pants, I don't... I really don't think I'll last if you get naked."

Cyrus laughs, his gums consuming his grin, eyes disappearing in cute little crinkles; And Anton feels his heart swoop through his belly. Fuck he's beautiful. They struggle for a moment, individually, shifting their pants down their legs and kicking them off. Putting those godforsaken things back on later will be an ordeal, but neither cares to focus on that just now. They both crawl back on the bed, to their prior positions, and pause. Anton startles Cyrus a little when he leans over, slowly, and kisses his cheek. He jerks back immediately, hands itching and skin clammy.

"Wow..." Cyrus exhales.

"Yeah... Wanted... Wow..."

"Tony?"

"Mm?" Anton stares into the distance, processing everything that's happening. His body is repelling the contact at the same time it's pulling it in, like magnets bouncing around each other... or maybe like a sink as it drains. He can feel his pulse everywhere.

"I changed my mind. I want... All I can think about right now is kissing you."

Anton turns, locking eyes with him, and smirks. "Even though we have no pants, that's what you're thinking about?"

"The only thing I'm gonna tell you right now..."

"Not... Not yet... I'm sorry Cy, that-"

"No, stop! Don't apologize. Your pace is my pace, remember? Tell me what you want baby. We'll do that."

Anton licks his lips and bites onto his bottom one, closing his eyes. Without a word, he slides his own hand down his body, cupping his half-hard cock gently. He hears Cyrus's faint curse, which goes straight to his own dick as it twitches.

He squeezes himself, feels the stiffness growing, and exhales with a puff. "Cy…"

"M'right here Tony… See for yourself baby… Everything you do… I will do okay?"

Cyrus's eyes are trained on Anton's lips, flicking down to his hand and up to his eyes periodically. He's desperately trying to take in every single thing about this moment that he can as he palms his own erection. He's already fully hard, aching for more. Anton nods and tugs on himself, groaning as his hips swirl in little circles like before. With his eyes closed, it's so easy to pretend Cyrus is touching him instead. Especially when he feels the warm puffs of air coming from the elder.

"Talk… talk to me?"

"Sure… You're so pretty like this baby. I wish that was my hand, holding you so tightly."

"Nnn… tight, yeah" Anton adjusts the pressure as he strokes himself leisurely, squeezing a little more. "Fuck…"

"Look at my hand, Tony. Watch me baby… Watch what you do to me"

Anton complies immediately, eyes dropping to where Cyrus strokes himself in time to his own hand. "Holy shit… Look at your hand… so pretty"

Cyrus flushes at the compliment, exhaling a breath he was holding. It comes out with a soft groan that sends Anton's hips kicking. Anton's gaze is heavy, it presses on Cyrus like he's sitting on top of him and ohhh... that sounds good.

"Imagining you sitting *ahh* on top of me..."

"I'd crush you"

"No baby, I'm so strong. You'd feel so good on top of me. Strong, firm, warm."

"Warm, yeah... I feel so warm with you..."

　　"Mmm. I'd love to run our cocks together... just like this" Cyrus twists his wrist, leaving the far side of his cock exposed, fingers held loosely open like he was holding another, unseen. Anton can see it, imagines his own fitting right there in that space.

"I'd like that. Someday, yeah?"

"Yes. Someday. Whenever you want."

"I... I want to taste you, too..."

"Shit" Cyrus's hips leave the bed, head falling backwards.

Anton has the audacity to giggle. "Cute... so pretty..."

　　He looks at the creamy expanse of Cyrus's exposed neck and groans. He wants to taste that, too. He imagines it would feel warm, like his cheek was. Wonders if he would feel his pulse through it too.

　　"Wanna... Wanna lick your neck Cy... Is that what you meant? Ah, tasting every inch?"

"Y-yeah baby... Wanna lick you like a lollipop honestly." Cyrus opens his eyes and looks up at Anton, both of them panting as their hands move in sync.

"Yeah? Which *ah* which part of me?"

Cyrus's chuckle is low in his throat, sending light vibrations across the bed. "Every fucking part. Head to toe baby. My own personal candy."

"Might... might get a cavity, there's a lot of me."

They laugh, briefly, and then the air of silence surrounds them again. The only sounds are their breaths coming ragged and the increasingly wet sounds of their hands on their cocks.

"Wait, hang on..." Cyrus whispers, getting up and kneeling on the bed, facing Anton.

"What-"

"Shh, lay where I was. Trust me, okay?"

"I do... I do" Anton replies, doing as instructed. He can feel the body heat leftover from Cyrus and goosebumps break out all over his skin at the thought that this... is like a second hand hug, isn't it? He's... so warm. So so warm, a little cold on the edges where Anton is bigger.

Cyrus takes Anton's place, carefully laying on his side and angling his brace to be out of the way and under his head.

"Like this baby... Can you do this comfortably?"

Anton nods and carefully gets into position, accepting the pillow between his arm and head that Cyrus nudges over.

"Watch" Cyrus whispers, scooting closer. He scoots until he's inches away, and then starts stroking his own face, trailing his fingers leisurely across his nose, cheeks, and lips. He grins when Anton's face goes slack, eyes zeroed in on his hands.

"Good boy, keep watching okay"

"Nnng" is all Anton can say.

Cyrus swirls a finger around his mouth, lips parted and wet, before flicking his tongue out and licking at the tip of it. Anton chokes on a moan and Cyrus can feel his cock twitch against the bed beside him. It twitches so close to Cyrus's own... Good, yes. He lets his eyelids fall a little, open just enough to still watch Anton's reactions, and lets his mind drift to sucking and licking on his finger like it's the cock he wishes it was. After a moment, he adds a second finger, letting his tongue split the two digits. Before wrapping around the both of them, stroking his fingers with his tongue, head bobbing. He moans and his eyes fall shut briefly. They fly open when he feels motion near his hips.

Anton has brought a hand down and is stroking himself loudly.

"You licked your hand, didn't you baby?"

He gets a grunt in response, and he groans.

"Give... give me your hand. Bring it up here."

As soon as Anton's hand hovers near him, he sits up a little, angles his head, and spits right into his palm.

"Holy fuck. Holy... fuck... Cy..." Anton's heart feels like it's racing out of his chest as the heat blooms in his belly. It's tight, coiling around and around, and he gasps to fill his lungs with air. This... is incredible.

"Use it, Tony. Touch yourself with me. Spread me all over your pretty cock yeah?"

   "Fuckkk...." Anton's head lolls as he does so, the spit still warm as it touches his skin. Warm, and now slick, his hand flies across his cock loudly.

"That's it... keep going Tony. Doing so good for me, aren't you?"

"Y-yeah... fuck you feel so *good*"

"Mm... Bet you feel good too don't you? Wanna ride your thighs... They're so thick"

"Yeah? You... mmm you can do that sometime. I'll... I'd like that."

"Bet you would. Want me to climb you like the tree you are, don't you?"

"Yeah... shit yeah."

   Anton grunts, his hips now rocking to meet the thrusts of his hand. With one particularly strong thrust, the head of his cock touches Cyrus's hands and they both still instantly.

   Sparks are flying beneath the skin of them both, but Anton's are igniting especially hot in his core. "I just..."

   "Yeah" Cyrus replies, out of breath. "You okay? We can... we can stop if you-"

"No! No... Wanna... Can I?"

Cyrus pulls his hand away from himself and looks into Anton's eyes. "Tell me. Tell me what you want baby I'll do it. I mean it. This is about you."

"Don't... Don't move. I want to... um..." Anton swallows and looks down at their swollen members, watches as they leak from their tips. "Wanna touch but no hands..."

"Shit... God yeah, okay. I will stay still... take what you need..."

Anton nods and rocks his hips forward experimentally. He misses the first time, frowns, and rocks again. Their cockheads touch, briefly, causing Anton to moan loudly. "Holy fuck..."

Cyrus bites his lip and squeezes his core, desperately trying to lay still.

"I'm not gonna move but... Can I tell you what I think? What I... What I picture?"

"Please" Anton exhales, still concentrating on where their cocks rest against the bed.

"Wanna push you back and swallow you whole. Wanna press your thick cock right up against my belly, and ride you."

"Fucking hell Cy" Anton's hips jerk again, missing Cyrus's cock once more in excitement, and Anton grunts. He tenses and focuses where he's aiming, sliding their tips together again.

It's hot, it's electric, the way they slide against each other. Anton's cock is still a little wet with Cyrus's spit, and a whole lot wet with their mingling precum.

"More please..."

Anton's thrusting develops a rhythm, sweat beading on his brow as he concentrates. He's not even thinking about the fact that they're touching, like this, he's just chasing those tiny little sparks that rocket through him like a cold drink in summer.

"Wanna kiss your face... taste your lips... Wanna taste myself on your lips" Cyrus moans, imagining the salty sweet kiss. He feels Anton's cock kick at his own as he speaks.

"Can you move, Cy? Move your hips with me?"

"Yeah... anything baby" Cyrus whispers, watching Anton's face as he bucks his own hips towards him. "How's this?"

He grinds his hips forward, his own cock trapping Anton's between itself and the bed. A light pressure, but it feels like heaven to the younger. He closes his eyes, imagining how it would feel to have Cyrus's hand wrapped around him.

"Someday, this is gonna be my mouth baby. Gonna kiss your pretty cock just as much as I kiss your cute face."

"Yeah?"

"Mm. Gonna kiss every single inch of you, right down to your toes."

Anton laughs airily and finally looks up at the wrecked pink-flushed face of Cyrus. "Beautiful... You're so beautiful..."

Cyrus smiles back, eyes still half-lidded with arousal, and moans as their cocks glide against each other again. They both rut so far forward that their tips graze the others' bellies, and, fuck that's nice.

"You feel.. so good. S'always this good?"

    "No" Cyrus replies instantly. "No it is definitely not always this good."

"...oh"

"It's you baby. You make this so good."

Anton shakes his head, bucking a little faster as he chases his approaching climax. "N-no... never this good alone... it's you... it's us..."

"Yeah" Cyrus agrees, leaning closer to breath the same air Anton is exhaling. Anton notices and leans in, touching their foreheads softly. "Yeah it's us"

It's awkward, holding this head-touching, rutting their cocks together, without their bodies touching. But it works. It works even as Anton leans over and carefully grabs Cyrus's hand, lacing their fingers together again. Their hands squeeze, and tug, as they leverage their hips against the rolling motions, but their heads never separate. Even as their hips lose their rhythm, even as Cyrus finds himself squeezing Anton's hand in warning, they stay pressed forehead to forehead.

    "Baby... I... I am so close" Cyrus whines softly, keening in his throat as the sparks threaten to explode.

        "Do it... cum for me please... Let me feel you... Let me feel you all over me pleeease... Please please"

Anton begs so prettily that Cyrus's head tilts, brushes their noses together accidentally, as he tips over the edge, moaning lowly. "Fuck baby... Beg so pretty..."

    The second Anton feels Cyrus's cum streak across his belly, and their cocks, he gasps. His eyes shoot open, taking in the pink cheeks, red lips, fluttering dark lashes of Cyrus as his mouth falls open in bliss. It's too much. It's so much and not enough, and Anton doesn't know what he's supposed to do. So he takes a breath and does what his gut says. He squeezes Cyrus's hand tighter, pulls it closer to his own body, not touching just enough to feel him closer. And then, the coil of heat and sparks and fire that has been building in his body snaps and his eyes white out, sparks shooting from his belly to his cock, and then back again through his limbs. As he feels his release shooting out of him, he follows his instinct.

It's scary, but he refuses to keep this bubble he's had. He can't go back now, not now that he knows what this is like. What love feels like.

So he tilts his head, and snares Cyrus's parted lips with his own.

Anton feels the moment Cyrus registers what is happening. He feels his jaw go slack and his body go stiff. He feels the way the bed shivers a little from Cyrus's body clenching. And as he looks into Cyrus's eyes, he sees the shock swirling.

"Relax. I'm trying not to overthink this, I can't convince you not to do the same okay?"

"Yeah" Cyrus whispers against his lips "Right, got it. Not overthinking. Can I like normal-think it though?"

Anton chuckles a little, nudging their noses together. "Sure, that's fine"

"Wow... I-" Cyrus opens and closes his mouth a few times, clearly unable to figure out what he wants to say.

"Yeah... It felt right. S'okay?"

"Yes! Yes. Very okay. Mhm." Cyrus nods rapidly, breath ghosting across Anton's face like a warm breeze.

"Can I be honest?"

"Please do, so I stop thinking too much"

Anton giggles, before continuing. "I can't explain why, but... With you, I want to fight whatever it is that holds me back. I... With Josh and Jamie here, I was so nervous, but when it's just us, I feel like I... Like my brain kind of turns off?"

"Not... fully off obviously just... Like I don't have to think as hard. Like I-"

"Like you're safe?"

"Yes. Very safe."

"Taken care of?"

"Absolutely."

"Like you're being protected, instead of having to protect everyone else?"

Anton exhales with a quick huff. "How do you know exactly what I feel?"

"Because baby... that's love. That's how you make me feel."

"Really? I don't, you know, make you feel like you're in danger any given second of the day?"

"Not even for a half of a second."

"Even though, technically, you did get hurt because of me?"

"Me getting hurt around you doesn't mean you were the cause. If you weren't standing there with me, to push me out of the way, I would have been hit by the moped, and I'd be way more hurt than I am. And, before you argue that I wouldn't have been distracted, or wouldn't have even been out there, I will concede that's true. But I told you before, and I'll say it again. Life means getting hurt. If you live without getting hurt-"

"You live in a bubble that doesn't exist" Anton finishes for him.

"Exactly. I'm not saying your choice to try and live in that bubble is a bad one, but... It's not the life for me. I want to enjoy myself, have meals with friends, tackle someone to the ground for a hug maybe, I dunno. I want to show that I love the people around me, not just tell them. Because that's how they feel like you do right now. Safe, warm, happy, protected."

"Loved..."

"And loved, yes."

"I love you, Cy... I know I can't show it, like everyone else yet but-"

"I'm gonna stop you right there. You do show it. Showing love is not the same for everyone. Josh shows love by touching, true. To a degree, Jamie does too. But you know what? I don't. Not always. I show my love in other ways too. Can you recall them?"

Anton frowns, pouts his bottom lip out a moment as he thinks. He doesn't have to think long, because he immediately thinks of their first encounter.

"You picked up my books... checked on me, brought me down from panic."

"Go on"

He thinks to their next few encounters.

"You helped me get back into my room... Walked between me and the crowd... Kept my mind on things that mattered... You"

Anton's eyes water a little as he thinks of all the tiny ways Cyrus has said 'I love you' over the last couple of weeks.

"You gave me the last piece of f-food, and you moved things in your room so I wouldn't b-be scared of breaking them, and you-"

Cyrus leans forward to kiss him, waiting for permission. Anton's tears start to slide down his cheeks as he nods and Cyrus softly presses their lips together.

"I love you, baby. All of those are how I love you. I love you by giving what I can to make things easier for you. I love you by making your path a little bit easier. I love you by giving you what you need, to do everything yourself, your way. I love you the way you deserve to be loved. The way you should be loved. The way I wish I could have loved you for years so you never had to fight these demons alone."

Anton nods against Cyrus' face, chest catching as he sobs a little. "I can tell. I-I think that's why I feel so safe. It's not that I know you'll catch me... I know you would... But I... I feel so strong with you. Strong like I always wished I was."

"You always were, you just didn't realize it. That's all I'm doing baby. Helping you realize how fucking strong you already are."

Anton nods again, reaching out slowly to curl a finger around Cyrus' hair.

"I can't promise I'm better. I-I can't picture touching anyone else like this… But with you… For you… I wanna try."

"Baby steps. Your pace is my pace, yeah?"

"Yeah."

The familiar silence creeps back, as they nose against each othercarefully.Neitheroneissureentirelyofwheretheboundary will fall, but neither is willing to purposely put it back up either.

After a few minutes, Cyrus snorts. "Gonna suck putting those pants back on one-handed…"

"We'll help each other… And, um… I have sweats if you want to borrow some. Better than jeans…"

"Can we shower first? Maybe change the sheets?"

"Definitely. Together?"

"Together."

Music room the next day

Jamie joined Josh and Cyrus in the music room, for dance practice. Cyrus watched as his two best friends twirled and leapt around, the sound of their feet echoing loudly across the wooden floor. When they paused, limbs sprawled, to rest on the ground for a while, he scooted over and sat with them, quietly passing cold water bottles. He wanted to talk about Anton, but he also didn't want to be that guy in a relationship.

You know, the one that never shuts up about their partner, making them the center of every single conversation. He wanted to, but he definitely didn't want to as well, especially if it would make his friends uncomfortable.

Jamie nudges Josh while Cyrus is frowning at his own water. They share a look and Josh smiles.

"So, how'd it go after we left hmmm?" He asks, wiggling his brows suggestively.

When Cyrus flushes bright pink and still doesn't look up, Josh gasps.

"Wait, I was just teasing you... did you guys actually-"

"No! No, not... I mean not no, but not yes... It's complicated."

Jamie flops onto his belly, legs kicking in the air behind him. "Soooo what'd you do? Talk for 6 hours about your hopes and dreams?"

"Mm..." Cyrus looks up, smirking a little. "We didn't really get to the deep stuff. Not really. Busy doing... other things..."

"Oh my god our little Cyrus got virtually laid in person" Jamie laughs.

"Little? I'm your Elder you little shit"

"Doesn't change that you're little" Josh winks and nudges Cyrus' side.

"So go on, what'd you wanna talk about?"

"Ahh... M'that obvious?"

Josh and Jamie enthusiastically agree in tandem, and Cyrus sighs.

"Sorry... I just... I can't help but feel like I can help him, you know? Not like some kind of pet project, or in an 'I can fix him' way, not really, but like... Like..." He hesitates, trying to find the words.

"Like you can offer a perspective he needs, but can't see on account of his own walls."

"Yes. God, yes that."

Josh hums. "Yeah, I get it. I feel the same way about him. I also wanted to go back to our neighborhood, and apologize to his mother. But would that be overstepping?"

"Well" Jamie starts "It's not like you're butting into Anton's business per se... More clearing the air about your own, in regards to your parents' actions right? Trying to make right something that involves you. It involves him too, sure, but you know."

"Right, it's still your business. So you can't really intrude there, can you?" Cyrus reasons.

"Still... I'd feel a little better if we could convince Anton to come back with us. Or... you know at least to give the green light?"

Cyrus nods and Jamie hums, sipping water.

"Yeah, I think asking him first is the best option. Most polite for sure.Actually,I'mfreethenexttwoweekends,whataboutyou guys?"

Josh breaks out a colourful day planner, and flips through the pages. "Ahh I'm booked next weekend. Volunteering to teach a class down at the community center. Good the next though. Jamie?"

Jamie shrugs nonchalantly and says, "I'm fine with that."

Cyrus raises a brow. "Shouldn't you check?"

"Nah"

"What if you have something set up?"

Jamie shrugs again. "Then I'll reschedule it."

Before Cyrus could speak again to rebut, Josh claps a hand on Jamie's shoulder and exclaims, "Okay, UP we're going from the 4th verse, ¾ speed let's GOOO"

Cyrus quickly moves back to the piano bench, whipping out his phone to text Anton about their plans. He doesn't bother waiting for a response, just pockets his phone and slides his fingers onto the ivory keys in front of him.

The *ding* of a phone going off interrupted the exam. Anton's face went hot as he realized it was his phone, but he ignored it. No phones allowed out or it was automatic failure and would be listed as an attempt to cheat.

Thank the gods it was only a text, and not a phone call.

Anton quickly scribbled in the bare minimum answers, that he knew were technically correct just lacking his usual "Enthusiasm" as the professors put it, in his explanations. Whatever. He'd pass with absolutely soaring colours as usual. If there was one thing in this life he was confident about, it was his academic prowess. So, once he passed over the exam to the teacher's aide, he quietly shuffled his bag onto his shoulders and left the room.

The second his feet hit the hallway, he dug his phone out and swiped to open the screen. He felt his heart fly to his throat as the "Cy" ID popped up.

Oh.

Oh that's... Not what he expected to see.

Anton inhales deeply, exhaling slowly, before tapping on his phone to open his calendar app.

'Next weekend... next weekend... Oh, I have... Oh no... Well, that should be... Fine? Right? Yeah, probably.'

Sliding his fingers over, tapping twice, he hits 'call' on Cyrus's number.

"Hey! I'm out of my exam, just wanted to reply on my way back to my room."

"Oh good! I'm sure you did well, but good luck with the results all the same."

"Thanks. So, about your text..."

"Right, yeah. Is that okay? Josh is willing to go alone some other time if you would prefer..."

"No no, it's fine. Um, I'll actually already be heading home that weekend?"

"Oh? Is everything alright?"

"No, yeah, it's fine! It's just um... There's maybe kind of a tiny uh..."

        Anton whispers the last bit, and Cyrus presses his phone to his ear unseen to him.

"Sorry what was that Tony?"

        "Ahhhh... Well it's a family reunion... We're getting together to do... you know, family things. Meet the new cousins... make food... flaunt accolades... The usual..."

        "Oh! Oh wow okay... So, should we reschedule? I can tell-"

        "No no, actually... I think it'd be nice. To um... To have you. All of you."

        "Are you sure? Baby I don't mind, I'm sure they won't either..."

        "Yeah, I'm sure." Anton leans on the doorframe of his room, sighing softly. "Honestly, I hate going to these normally. I'm always
pretty on edge... you know... Lots of hot things, new babies, hand-shakes to avoid..."

"Ahhh I seeeee. You want me as your emotional support animal, while Josh and Jamie stun everyone into forgetting about you, is that right?"

Anton chuckles and slides his key into the handle.

"Actually, you nailed it yes. So...?"

        Cyrus smiles as he slides his fingers around the piano keys, the sounds of the room behind him long forgotten.

"Yeah. Yeah I think that's fine. Should we, I dunno, bring anything?"

        "I am pretty sure my family will take care of it... they usually bring enough for damn near the whole town if I'm honest."

"Okay... Okay wow I haven't even officially asked you to be my boyfriend and I'm already meeting your family. This is... wow..."

Anton grins, laying on his bed with a buzz on his lips, missing how Cyrus's felt on them already.

"Yep. Wow. Also yes, I thought that was obvious?"

"Ahhh come on Tony lemme ask properly okay?"

Anton sighs then, cast awkwardly laying across his belly.

"Sure, sure. You coming over tonight?"

"Yeah, we both absolutely need showers, and your bed makes way less noise than mine..."

"Ah, so this is what it feels like to be used for what I offer. Be still my heart, it pains me so"

Cyrus giggles at Anton's dramatic soliloquy, shaking his head.

"I... " He leans close to the piano to whisper, "IloveyouTony"

"...Love you, too. See you later."

"See you"

A loud "BYE TONYYYYY" echoes behind Cyrus as the call disconnects, leaving both boys flushed and warm.

Two weeks later

The quartet of friends opted to rent a car for the weekend, seeing as they weren't sure how long they would be around, and public transport would limit when they could make plans. And if it was a little more relaxing for Anton to sit in the back seat holding Cyrus's hand while Josh drove and Jamie sat in the front seat, then, all the better, right?

Anton leaned forward, guiding Josh through the streets to his home.

"I know the area, I just never knew where your house was. You weren't all that far away from me, were you Ton?"

Shaking his head, Anton laughs. "Might sound silly now, but back then I uh... I'd always hoped for a friend right next door, so I could do that telephone thing with cans."

He leans back, face looking morose. "Guess I should have lowered my expectations to just having a friend at all, eh?"

"Yah!" Josh starts, but Jamie waves him off, shaking his head.

"Shh, let him be. He knows, man."

Josh pinches his lips together, two little creases forming above them, but turns back to the front to finish parking the car.

Cyrus rushes, as soon as Josh has parked, to open the door for Anton. He smiles as his beau leans down to kiss him on the head before taking his hand.

"Thanks."

The two of them turn, waiting for Josh to grab his package from the trunk. He insisted on arriving with gifts, despite Anton's strong protesting.

'It's not about greeting with a gift, per se, it's just that I feel I owe you and your mother a lot... considering what my parents did. I can't show up empty handed Tony. I just can't.'

So, he'd prepared a beautiful many-layered honey and pistachio baklava cake for her, decorated with little violets and crumbled pistachios. He was going to bring some wine as well, but Anton managed to talk him down from it.

'I assure you, the uncles will bring plenty of liquor. The good stuff even.'

Josh inhaled, squaring his shoulders, as he braced himself for the confrontation. He hadn't seen Anton's mother in years, but he hoped she was as kind still as she seemed then.

Julia opened the door as they approached, drawn by their chatter.

"My baby! Oh my, you said you were bringing friends, I didn't realize they were all going to be so handsome! Come in, I'm Julia, Anton's mom."

Jamie went first, charismatic as usual, blinding her with a crescent-shaped eye smile as he bowed respectfully.

"It's a pleasure to meet you, my name is Jamie Williams"

"Williams? Are you related to-"

"I would actually be that kid ma'am" He interrupted her with a smirk, winking at Anton and stepping inside as ushered.

"I'm Josh Daniels, ma'am" Josh bowed as best he could with the cake, squaring his shoulders once more as he stood straight again. "And, I would like to formally apologize in the stead of my parents. Not on their behalf, as they don't know I'm here, but..."

"Apologize? Whatever could you be here to apologize to me for? I just hope you've healed well, young man. I should apologize to you again-"

Josh also interrupted her, shaking his head rapidly. "No no, please don't. Please, allow me to explain inside?"

Julia frowned, but nodded, ushering him in as well. When she turned back with a smile again to greet the final friend, she froze. Her eyes darted down, to the joined hands between Anton and Cyrus, and then up to Anton's face.

"T-Tony?"

His voice, barely over a whisper, came out with a breath. "Hey mom... This... This is Cyrus. He's very... special... to me..."

Cyrus squeezed his hand in reassurance before removing his hand to bow properly to his mother.

"Pleasure to meet you ma'am, I am Cyrus Matthews."

"...oh." Julia breathed out shakily, swallowing quickly. "My god okay. Tony you're- Cyrus is- Wow. Wow alright. P-please, come in, we have... We have so much to discuss, I think."

Cyrus steps inside the house quickly, leaving Anton alone with his mother for a moment. Anton looks anxious, stepping forward once... twice... The gap is closed with the next step. Julia is tense, eyes wide, as Anton's body heat hits her. She hasn't felt the warmth of her son since before her accident, and not a day had gone by that she hadn't thought about the saying... 'At some point you picked up your child for the last time, and didn't know it would be the last time'. At some point, she'd touched him... held him... hugged him... for the last time. She had spent many nights, many stars at night, wishing she could have known so she could have taken advantage of it. Cherished it more.

Anton wipes his sweaty hands on his pants before holding them out, fingers forward, towards his mother. She just stares down at his hands, brow furrowed, not understanding. So, he bends. He reaches down, fingers trailing across the back of her frail-looking wrists, sliding down to her palms. He gently lifts her hands into the space between them, squeezing gently. As he does so, her eyes go even wider, flicking between their hands and his face.

"Tony....TonyI-What-How-"

   "Cyrus is more special to me than you know, mom." His eyes well with tears, matched by his mother's own, as he smiles deeply. "He's so, so, so special."

"You're better?" She whispers, nervously.

Anton shakes his head a little, with a rueful look. "No, not completely. But I'm... I'm trying. He's helping."

"He's... is he a doctor? Or something?"

Anton laughs a little, running his thumbs over her knuckles. "No, nothing like that. He's just... Someone that loves me. Someone that I love."

"...Oh. Oh... Okay... Wow..." She exhales again, eyes widening when Anton leans forward suddenly and kisses her cheek.

"I missed you, mom. I missed you so much."

"Oh my god Tony" Her cheeks floor with tears that can't be contained anymore, relief and love and so many years of pent up feelings for her only son filling them. "Can I... Can I hug you?"

Anton flinches, wary, relaxing only when she steps back and holds up her hands.

"I won't! It's okay darling, I just-I'm-I just can't believe you've..." She chokes on her words, wiping at her tears quickly. "Sorry, sorry..."

Anton smiles softly and gestures for her to enter first. When he steps in, he's met immediately with a grinning Cyrus, who whispers conspiratorially into his ear as they lock fingers again.

"I can see you take after your mother emotionally then, hm?"

"Hey be respectful!"

Cyrus grins broadly, squeezing his hand. "I mean that in the best way baby. The best."

In their little bubble, they don't see the others watching them with matching smiles.

Josh sidles into the kitchen with Julia, presenting the cake for her and asking if she's alright to have a short conversation with him. She nods, carefully moving the cake to the fridge, before escorting him to an empty room down the hall.

With his mother indisposed, Anton is left responsible for welcoming guests. A few aunties shuffle in, arms laden with food and bags of who-knows-what, before a familiar face arrives.

"Tyler! It's been so long, come in!! Oh, who's this?"

Tyler steps into the house, fingers waggling in the air at Anton who mirrors the gesture, followed closely by a devilishly handsome man.

"I am Colt Owens, you must be Anton? Tyler has told me all about his favourite cousin" Colt bows, hair flopping across his forehead.

Anton laughs, stepping aside before bowing in return. "I am, I am. It's nice to meet you as well Colt. How do...?"

Tyler speaks then, arms lacing around Colt's bicep, body leaning against him with a dreamy look in his eyes. "He's my partner. We're hoping to get married abroad."

"Oh! Wow, congratulations! Welcome to the family, Colt please come in and sit with us!"

As Anton ushers them to sit with his friends, since they're all roughly the same age and the aunties have banished anyone in their age group from helping thus far, he leans towards Colt discreetly.

"Your name sounds familiar, did you grow up in this area too?"

Colt hums a little, wiggling his palm sideways. "Ehh kind of? My father used to work in a hospital near here. I followed his footsteps and took over his patients when he retired recently."

"You're a doctor then? That's amazing, you're so young!"

Anton and Colt scoot a little closer, so as to not interrupt the others with their own conversation. Tyler has latched himself onto Jamie, and the two are enthusiastically gesturing about something, with Cyrus looking on fondly.

"Ahh, I actually originally wanted to be a tattoo artist when I first went to school." Colt slides his sweater sleeve up his arm to reveal dozens of tattoos pieced together in a beautiful image.

"Whoa, those are beautiful. What changed your mind?"

Colt shrugs then, glancing at Tyler. "I guess I found a reason to want something a little less crazy and a little more stable?"

Anton follows his gaze before his own lands on Cyrus. "You know, I think I get it."

They look back at each other and laugh, leaning back to watch their partners for a while in comfortable silence.

The first to break it is Colt a few minutes later, who flips his lip ring back and forth in thought. "Do you mind if I ask you something? Ah, personal?"

"Sure, I don't mind at all."

"It's just... Tyler told me about your... thing with touch. Can I ask?"

"Ah, that. What um... What exactly do you want to know?"

"Well, why do you not like it? When did it start? What... Sorry, it's probably none of my business I'm just... I guess I'm curious more than anything" He finishes, laughing nervously.

Anton hums thoughtfully before answering. "I wouldn't say I don't like touch. I just... I've always seen myself as a bit of a curse, I suppose. Everyone I've ever touched has ended up hurt as a direct result of it." He raises a hand when Colt looks to argue, shaking his head a little. "I know, I know. It doesn't make sense. Except, it does. Jamie there, when we first met I split his lip with a book I was holding, then broke his nose when I bowed in apology.

He ran away from me, as he should have. Josh, you haven't met him yet, I broke his ribs hugging him with our introduction. At least, I thought I did. Turns out he had a fracture already from dancing, but even still... My hug hurt him because of that. If I hadn't hugged him, you know?"

Anton sighs, face contorting into one of pain as he recalls the worst of them all.

"And, as for when... I avoided touch as much as I could, watching my step, trying not to break more things, all my life really. Growing up I saw myself as why my dad was gone, why things got broken, why people got hurt. So, I did everything I could think of to... mitigate that. Walked slower, ate less, stayed away from others. I figured all I needed... was my mom. As long as I had her to come home to, to fall into her arms, I was safe. She came home from work one day, from her second or third job of the day, with a cold. It was a bad one, she could barely stand for the whole week without grabbing onto something. Dizzy, I guess? Anyway. I made us tomato soup that night. So she wouldn't have to. I stubbed my toe on the table, because of course I did, and turned to put the pot there. She was there, and..."

Anton chokes a little, hands squeezing each other tightly. Colt instinctively reaches out to console him, but moves his hand to his own leg instead. "Hey, you don't have to say anything else... I'm sorry I asked..."

"N-no it's okay. I... I want to tell you."

As Anton looks up, blinking away the tears pooling, he realizes the other three have turned to him during his story, and are intently listening. He inhales, hands squeezing tighter until his knuckles have gone white.

"I tripped or something, I-I don't remember exactly. All I remember is looking at the pot, being so careful with stepping on

my injured toe and not wanting to drip hot soup over the edge...
And then I saw my mom standing in a pool of red and...”

Cyrus scoots over, kneeling down to grasp Anton's hands in his
own. “I'm right here, baby. I'm here, okay?”

“We ended up in the hospital. She... She had burns all over her
legs, had to be wrapped all over. The doctor, he said they found a
fracture in her foot, too. I couldn't just burn her, I had to drop the
pot on her foot too. Was weeks before she could go back to work”

Anton sniffs, reaching a hand up to wipe at his face before
shrugging. “I decided then, I wouldn't touch anyone else. I
wouldn't... I wouldn't hurt anyone else ever again.”

“Hang on... Did you say a foot fracture? What's... what's your
mother's name, Anton?”

“Julia? Julia Richards, why?”

“Oh my god... Richards?!”

“Yes? Why?”

Colt leans forward, looking at Anton with wide, serious eyes.
“Anton, you... You weren't responsible for your mother's foot. And
her burns were superficial, they were probably healed within a
couple of days.”

“I-No? I don't remember some details, but I can assure you her
foot was broken, and she was in the hospital after the burns for a
couple of weeks. I am completely sure of that.”

“No! I mean, yes, she was in the hospital for that long, but not
for the burns. It was her foot, technically, but she volunteered to
stay.”

"She... wanted to stay?" Anton's thoughts start spiraling quickly, almost immediately. Did she choose to stay away from him? Was she that scared of him?

Cyrus squeezes his hand, shaking his head at him to say 'don't'.

Colt continues, quickly. "Yes. She... Okay so I don't have the paperwork here obviously, but when I took over my dad's patients I got a look at a lot of his old records. And, your mother's injury was listed as a workplace one."

"Work...place?"

"Yes, as in she obtained the injury as a result of her workplace. Not you."

"I don't... understand... The pot hit the floor, are you sure it didn't-"

"I don't know about that, but I know she listed the injury as workplace-related, and that she volunteered to extend her stay until it healed enough to return to work."

Anton looks up and catches his mother's gaze, Josh shifting awkwardly beside her.

"...You thought... All this time my darling you thought... Oh my god..."

Julia breaks down into tears, falling onto the floor in front of Anton. "My baby you thought you hurt me? Y-you stopped... Oh my god Tony I am sorry, mom is so sorry."

"I... didn't? I watched... Seeing you in that cast, and bandaging, and in s-so much pain... Mom I couldn't... I couldn't do that again... It h-hurt so bad seeing you hurt like that b-because of me..."

She shakes her head back and forth rapidly, reaching her hands out hesitantly. "No, no no no baby. Not you, never you, please..."

"If I didn't th-then how? Why?"

Josh, seated now beside Jamie, speaks up. "That... would be me, actually. Indirectly, anyway..."

The other heads swivel towards him, faces full of questions, so he smiles grimly and continues.

"When my parents lied about my rib injury, they pushed blame onto you guys. I can't speak for them as to why they did, but they did. Your mom wanted you to finally have a friend, and she'd seen how happy we were, so she...She agreed."

Anton looks between Josh and his mother, who still sobs quietly at his feet. He reaches a shaky hand out to hold hers and she grips it like a lifeline as Josh keeps talking.

"Well, she couldn't afford the high payments that my parents asked for, for my 'continued medical care'. Your mom worked extra jobs to make sure she could make those payments. I found out not long ago, when I found the letters. My parents, they never even opened those letters. I wish they had. Your mom loves you so much, those letters... Fuck, sorry..." He pauses, lip quivering a little at the thought of what his parents put this family through.

"I'msorry.I'msosorryforeverythingthathappenedbecauseof me, because of my parents."

Julia leans over and grabs Josh's hand with her other one, a human lifeline between Josh and Anton, two friends that almost were. "No, don't apologize sweetie. It's not on you, I forgive you, like I said in there."

Josh smiles and pats the top of her hand. "I appreciate it, but I will be spending so many years of my life apologizing to you both."

"So..." Jamie speaks softly, "Another misunderstanding."

Anton looks up and nods, taking a deep breath to steel himself.

"Can I... Can I ask a favour of you guys? This is gonna sound crazy..."

"Anything you want, Ton" Jamie whispers, not wanting to upset him further.

"Can you guys... Can you all hug me?"

There are a few gasps, with Colt glancing around awkwardly before asking, "Um, all of us?"

Anton nods and reaches out to put a hand on his shoulder, lips pinching at the contact. He could do this. For weeks all he'd heard was that the people around him got hurt near him, but not because of him, and even though the voice in his head was mostly silent... He couldn't shake the intrusive thought that kept coming up every single time he thought about the ways people showed physical affection with each other, wishing he could do the same.

Bandage. Like a bandage, or like a bubble bursting, it was time.

"Yes, all of you. Every one of you, please... All I ever wanted was to feel warm again... To feel loved again... To feel normal again... I know it'll take time to be okay with it all, but please..."

And then, he's piled and surrounded. Colt is surprisingly the first to reach out, arms reaching around him in a tight grip that is as firm as it is warm. His mother is next, enveloping the both of them, and then he can't count the bodies. He vaguely feels Cyrus's hands on his, steady. He sighs. His hands itch, and his brain has gone fuzzy, but he feels... warm. Definitely warm. He also feels the safest he thinks he has felt in maybe his whole life. A bit like a turtle that finally discovered what a shell is, and has found his own. A place to call home.

After what feels like years to Anton, he feels movement, and then another weight added behind him. The thrumming in his ears gets louder and his arms start to crawl with goosebumps, because he doesn't know who this is. Who is it? Who is touching? What if-

"Hey little brother, I didn't know we were doing hugs now?!"

Javier Phillips, Anton's eldest cousin, who had a soft heart for Anton and protected him most of his life.

"Oh, cuz, it's you." Anton's shoulders visibly unclenched, and Javier pulled away to pat his back soothingly.

"Sorry for assuming, just... You know I've asked for that your whole life..."

"No, no it's... I'm glad you did. Now... Now everyone I love really is here."

Anton leans back and looks to each person there. His mother. His cousins. Their loved ones. His loved ones. This, right here, was his family.

"You're my family. I have a family, and it's... it's you guys" He smiles even as a few more tears make their way down his cheeks, one catching on the dimple of his broad grin.

Javier laughed, loudly, sitting on the arm of the chair next to Colt, leaning on the man's shoulder comfortably. "Wow, and this is the first I'm hearing of it? Anton Phillips, my FAMILY?"

The group laughs, nervous energy breaking almost immediately. Anton's mother still has a hand on his knee, afraid to never get the chance again if she removes it, while Cyrus clutches one hand between his fingers in silent support. The aunties call for Julia, so she reluctantly pulls away. But not before Anton stands and pulls her into a tight hug, both arms swallowing her slight frame. She sobs and clutches at his back, squeezing him with everything she has.

"I love you Tony Bologna" She whispers, as he whispers back.

"I am so sorry. I love you mom"

The first day of the reunion goes quickly, filled with greetings and hustling of ingredients into the kitchen. Tubs are washed and crocks are warmed, and everything is laid out for the next day of cooking and grilling.

Tyler and Colt get the main guest room, having pulled "couple priority" to get the claim in; But seeing as Tyler couldn't unlatch himself from Jamie, Josh and Jamie were quickly roped into joining their sleeping arrangement, with mats and blankets piled into one massive bed. Josh and Colt may have been shunted to the edges of the makeshift bed. But, they didn't mind. Watching the other two get along so well, so fast, warmed their hearts in a way they couldn't express in words.

Javier took the couch, since he was a last minute arrival. Most of the other rooms were filled with other family units, so as a single he was completely fine with his arrangement. Especially since it meant he would be able to spy on anyone up late.

Cyrus was quietly escorted to Anton's childhood bedroom, a private arrangement for the two of them, obviously.

The bed was small, but Cyrus secretly hoped that wouldn't be an issue tonight. He was aware of the possibility, considering how big of a day Anton had already had. So, he clutched at a pillow and hesitated while Anton shut the door and kicked his slippers off.

Anton sits on the bed, facing Cyrus, smiling up at the elder.

"Hey"

"Hey" Cyrus smiles back at him shyly.

Anton reaches forward and tugs the pillow away from him, tossing it somewhere on the bed. Pouting, Cyrus tries to grab it back, but Anton catches a wrist easily.

"You really want that raggedy thing instead of me to hold tonight?"

"Well... No... But-"

"But?" Anton's hands tug on Cyrus, pulling him to stand between his legs, heat radiating out of him. So much warmth. His fingers gently move to Cyrus's hips, squeezing lightly.

"But I... I didn't want to presume..."

"What, that on a day when I've touched more people than I have in my entire life, I wouldn't want to touch the man that made it happen?"

He shifts, hands pulling Cyrus by his thighs, and it's Cyrus's turn to shudder at the contact between them. His legs feel wobbly with the idea that his Anton is caressing him right now.

"Fuck, Tony, be careful…"

Anton blinks up at him, frowning. "You think I'm gonna hurt you? Shit, am I already?" he moves his hands back, away from Cyrus, just in case.

"No! Shit, no I mean-that's not…" Cyrus sighs and swallows hard before continuing. "I meant, be careful that you don't start something you can't finish tonight…"

"Oh?" Anton quirks an eyebrow.

Cyrus is unimpressed, lips pressed tight.

"And if I… want… to finish?" Anton retorts, pressing soft kisses to the front of Cyrus's belly as he spoke.

"Ahhhh… Tony please…"

"Cy, can I… Can I please touch you tonight?"

"Me? You don't want it the other way?"

Anton shakes his head, thumbs drifting beneath Cyrus's top to press against the skin of his hips. Cyrus closes his eyes, fighting the desperate urge to buck into Anton's touch. He could do it, right? Surrender to Anton? Lord knows he'd been practicing already…

"Okay… Yeah. You take control baby. Tonight… Tonight will be yours okay?"

"Mine hmm?" Anton lifts his shirt an inch to press a kiss to his belly right by his hip, breath ghosting across his skin softly.

Cyrus grunts, unable to speak, hands threading into Anton's hair.

"Will you be entirely mine, too?"

"Hnng?" Cyrus blinks down at Anton in confusion.

"Be mine... My lover, my fighter... My boyfriend. Will you be entirely mine?"

Cyrus gasps, brain short circuiting. He was supposed to ask, he was supposed to do it right, he was-

"Y-you're asking me..." It's not a question, he just breathes his realization and Anton chuckles.

"Yeah. M'asking because... You were taking too long... And I want to tell everyone I care about, about you. Wanna scream it really."

"Fuck... I just... I wanted to do it right, you know?"

"You just met my mom, my cousins, my whole family. What's more right than right now?"

Cyrus realizes he's right, this is the moment. This is the place. Where the pain all started, where Anton's first steps into loneliness and despair and the bleak reality he's had for more than a decade all happened. Yes, this is it.

And that's his answer.

He exhales, kneeling down to the floor to look up at Anton, hands grasping at his face. "Yes. Yes baby I will be your everything, as long as you'll be mine?"

Anton nods and makes quick work of easing his lips around Cyrus's. Fireworks spark in his belly immediately, and he moans.

"Fuck,Tony...Areyousure?Pleasegodstopnowifyou're not..."

He gets a chuckle in response, alongside hands sliding up his bare skin, lifting his shirt off.

"I'm sure, Cy. Want you... need you..."

"Holy fu-" Cyrus is cut off by a kiss once more, hands pulling on his elbows insistently. He climbs clumsily onto the bed, straddling Anton as the bigger man falls backwards, their lips separating only briefly.

Anton grunts before gently pushing him off, directing him to the head of the bed, carefully arranging pillows so he can be angled upwards and comfortable.

"Stay" Anton whispers, leaning back to look at his bare chest. "Fuck you're even more beautiful than I thought, you know that?"

Cyrus grins, biting his lip. "Thought about it a lot have you?"

He means it teasingly, but the darkness pooling in Anton's eyes sets him ablaze. "Yes. Every night since day one"

"Shit... really?"

"Mmn." Anton nods, fingers sliding up Cyrus's thighs to tug at his waistline.

"M-me too... Touched myself thinking of you... wishing it was you..."

"It is. It is me now"

"Yeah" Cyrus agrees, breathily. "Yeah it is... fuck"

Cyrus wants to touch, and hold Anton, but he promised to let him do the touching. So he clutches the sheets in both hands and squeezes, to have something to hold onto at least. Anton's fingers work quickly to open Cyrus's pants and slide them down his legs.

"You're like... Like porcelain. So fucking pretty... wow..."

"Heh... Don't be afraid to break me though baby. I can take it, I assure you."

Anton's hesitance flies out the window momentarily, as he leans up to catch Cyrus's lips again, whole body pressed against the elder's. He moans as heat floods his nerves, his mouth, his core. Everything feels so hot, everywhere.

"Hot... too hot..." He mumbles against Cyrus's lips, clutching at his own shirt. He pouts, causing a giggle to emanate from Cyrus in response.

"Want me to help?"

Still pouting, Anton nods, defeated by the shirt that has now snared and tangled his arms within it. Cyrus leans up, legs pressing against Anton's as he spreads them to anchor himself. As he tugs at Anton's shirt, he snakes his hands across his skin gently. Anton goes still, skin sparking as the feather-light touches flutter across him. "God" he whines, twisting between Cyrus's legs and throwing his shirt away the second he's free from it.

"Shh it's okay. I've got you baby" Cyrus whispers, peppering kisses down his face, then neck. Anton shivers and presses him backwards.

"Too much... Fuck too much..."

"Sorry"

"No, no, good too much, just, wan'touch you okay?"

"Sure, I'll behave" Cyrus leans back on the pillows and locks his fingers behind his head for good measure.

Anton licks his lips, unsure where he wants to start. He decides he wants to do what they talked about before, and scoots down the bed to kiss at Cyrus's bare feet. Cyrus giggles, legs clenching as he tries very hard to stay still as promised.

"Ahhh Tony... Feels good, but... but don't linger there kay"

He gets a grunt in reply as Anton works up to kiss at his calves, cradling his leg between his hands. "So pretty, Cy. So soft. So..."

"So?" Cyrus whispers, eyes fluttering as he tried to look down.

"So perfect. So, so, so perfect" Anton leans up and presses a kiss to his lips, bare chests softly rubbing against each other. Cyrus moans and brings his hands down to gently stroke at Anton's sides, relishing in the feeling.

"Cyyy"

"Sorry! Sorry baby just... I'll stop"

"No! I don't... I want you to keep going... please..."

"What are you feeling?"

Anton frowns, eyes pinched shut, trying to put it to words. It's so much, it's everything and yet he knows it's not much at all. He gasps when Cyrus swipes a thumb across a nipple experimentally.

"Fuck... Feels like fire. Fire that doesn't hurt. Feels like feathers too, but also... ahhh do that again holy fuck" Anton moans and throws his head back as Cyrus's tongue flicks against his throat. Cyrus obliges, and Anton all but keens, hips crashing down against his own.

"Nnng Tony... You taste so good..."

"Good as you expected?"

"Mmm better baby"

"You... Can I?" Anton looks down and Cyrus flushes hot. Anton looks so blissed right now, like his mind is entirely somewhere else.

"Please... Do anything you want baby. Anything you want to try okay?"

"Nng... What if it's weird?"

"Fuck, especially then are you kidding me?"

"You sure?"

"Your pace is my pace remember?"

"Shit.. kay... okay..."

Anton kisses him, harder than before, full of desperation, nipping at his lips harshly. His kisses slide down his throat before devolving into a glide of his tongue, tasting every inch of Cyrus he can reach. From his jaw to his ear, down to his collarbone, he tastes and tastes.

Cyrus bucks his hips at the sensations, aching for relief as the hot tongue is replaced with cool air from Anton's panting breaths.

"Tony... fuck I need your hands on me... please..."

"Where? Here?" Anton slides a hand to Cyrus's chest, fingertips tickling at his budding nipples before being replaced with his mouth.

Anton moans, the feeling of Cyrus under his fingers is electrifying, more so every time he hears him gasp at his ministrations. His hands are tingling, and the taste of him on his tongue is insane. Salty, sweet, indescribably Cyrus.

He shuffles up onto his knees and carefully shifts his own pants off, hesitating at his briefs. He catches Cyrus's wide eyes and waits, thumbs hovering at the waistline.

"Please, Baby. Let me see you, yeah?"

That's all the encouragement Anton needs. His thumbs drop, dragging the cloth down his legs, and when he stands to lean back onto the bed, he gasps when Cyrus's hand reaches for his cock carefully. It's just a finger, gliding from base to tip, least to most sensitive.

But, fuck, it feels good. He chokes on his moan, pressing his hips against Cyrus's venturing hand. "More, Cy... please"

"Come here, straddle me, yeah? Remember what we mentioned before?"

Anton nods and shuffles over carefully, hands bracing on either side of Cyrus's smaller body as he gently slips his legs on either side of him. Cyrus isn't fully exposed yet, but his briefs are straining against his own arousal, which comforts Anton.

He's glad he's not the only one feeling so affected, because it makes him feel... normal. Like a normal man in bed with his lover.

"Lover" he whispers, in awe, bending down to kiss Cyrus reverently. "You're my lover"

"Yes, baby... For as long as you'll have me" Cyrus's hands thread into his hair, pulling him down for a deeper kiss. It's smooth, and warm, and even with teeth clicking it's a kiss unlike any other. Anton's brain lights up with tingles, head fuzzy.

"More" He whispers into Cyrus's mouth as he cradles his head and neck in one broad hand. "More, please, I want so much more..."

"Can I give it? Or do you still want to take?"

"Mmn... Can you? It's so much, I don't know..."

"Shh it's okay. Lemme make you feel good, yeah?"

Anton nods, collapsing with a grunt to the bed beside Cyrus, who quickly shifts them so he's straddling Anton now. His legs are pale and soft against Anton's thick thighs, and he moans at the sight. "Fuck, your thighs are so thick baby..."

"Not today, but I'm absolutely going to ride them sometime okay?"

"Y-yes... I'd like that."

Anton glides his hands to Cyrus's hips, squeezing them, fingers dipping beneath the waist of his briefs. He pouts, bottom lip jutting out so sweetly that Cyrus has to taste it. When Cyrus finally pulls back, Anton is breathless with his request.

"Off? Wan'feel, please..."

"Yeah... one second"

Cyrus leans back, kicks the final remnant of clothing off and climbs back astride Anton's thighs. His cock bobs eagerly, dangerously close to Anton's already.

"God... it's so pretty... all of you is this pretty?"

"Ahh" Cyrus chuckles nervously, "Shh please... m'not that cute..."

"You are, you really really are." Anton's hands are back on him, squeezing his thighs as he waits for Cyrus to make the next move.

Cyrus scoots, spreads his legs a little wider, so his body is more flush against Anton's. Their cocks touch, briefly, and both of them moan softly. Anton is squeezing Cyrus's thighs tightly, tight enough to maybe bruise, and it's all Cyrus can do not to ask for more.

Because the idea alone of walking out of this room bearing marks, proof of Anton having him, has him leaking profusely over his body.

He thrusts his hips forward, letting their cocks graze each other, eyes glued to Anton's face to gauge how he takes the feeling. His own member kicks back against Cyrus involuntarily, but other than that Cyrus only sees a wide gaze of wonder.

"Tony... nnng put your hand around us both. L-like we talked about yeah?"

Anton nods and complies immediately, long fingers wrapping around the back side of Cyrus's cock, thumb and palm gripping the back side of his own. He moans, squeezing experimentally.

"Fuck, Cy it's…"

"So good, right baby? Hold tight okay"

"Nng… kay" Anton grips them tighter just as Cyrus starts to move his hips. He moves slowly, at first, more of a grinding than a thrusting, but it sparks along their nerves like lightning. The movement is inhibited a little by the lack of lube, but it's nice. It feels soft, in a way. Warm as the tightened friction increases, but soft. Cyrus pulls his hand palm-up and spits profusely into it, letting the last of the saliva drip slowly off his tongue. Anton moans beneath him, and Cyrus smirks.

"Remember how this feels baby?"

Anton nods frantically. "Mmhm"

"Want it again?"

"Please! Please please" Anton begs, unable to form another word as his brain screams to feel Cyrus's slick spit on his cock again.

Cyrus brings his hand down, sliding the warm spit across their cocks before wrapping his fingers over top of Anton's. He laces them together and strokes the top of Anton's thumb with his own. Together, they stroke slowly.

After a few moments, he feels Anton's hips kicking upwards instinctively, searching for more friction, so he licks his lips and lets his fingers drop down to tease their tips with each up stroke. The effect is immediate as Anton's moan echoes in the quiet room.

"Fuck... Tony you sound so hot..."

"Mmm... Cyrus, please..."

"Okay, hold on. Let me take care of you yeah?"

Anton nods with a pout, eyes glassy as his hand falls awkwardly to his belly. He watches as Cyrus crawls backwards, hands on either side of his hips, eyes focused on his spit-slicked arousal. Fuck, that is hot.

Hotter still when Cyrus leans forward, breath ghosting across the tip, and looks up into Anton's eyes waiting for the OK. Anton nods, throat bobbing, and then his body erupts into sparkling fire. Cyrus' mouth is on him, tongue hot and wet as it trails up and down the length of his cock slowly. It flicks across the tip, catching the precum oozing, and ignites something deep in Anton's belly. His hands clutch desperately at Cyrus's nape, squeezing.

"Hhh...nng" He rasps out, head thrown back.

"I'm here Tony" Cyrus reaches a hand up to tease Anton's belly, swirling his fingers up towards his nipple. As soon as Cyrus makes brief contact, his lover's body writhes, pushing his hips against his mouth. He opens wide, tongue hanging out, letting the tip slip inside.

With his other hand, he props himself up and angles his body to slip more of Anton's cock into his mouth, careful to go slowly in case he gets overwhelmed. The hands on his neck squeeze, one drifting to the crown of his head before pulling briefly. He starts to lift, sliding the warm cock from his lips, but the hand pushes then, shoving him down slowly. He grins and brings both hands down, tucking one underneath himself like a cat, allowing himself to bob leisurely with Anton's hand as a guide.

"You... you're so...mmhh...so good fuck" Anton is whispering a trail of thoughts, eyes squeezed shut as he allows himself to feel. His mind, for the first time in his life, feels absolutely blank outside of this moment.

Nothing exists but him, Cyrus, and the sensations rippling across his body. He strokes Cyrus's neck with his thumb, fingers grazing his neck lightly. Cyrus moans at the contact and tilts his head a little to give more access.

Grunting, Anton pulls him up and off his cock by the hair, pulling until he has to scoot his knees and straddle Anton again, face flush to his face.

"Cy... wanna fuck you... Can I?"

Cyrus's breath is ragged, head lolling under Anton's control. He tries to say yes, but all he manages is a fucked out 'ess'. Anton flips them with no grace at all, and dips his head down to Cyrus's cock as it bobs against his belly. He licks a wide stripe, kisses the tip...

And then his tongue falls down to his rim, winking pink in front of him. He kisses Cyrus's cheeks, fingers pulling them apart trying to reach what he really wants, before grumbling in frustration. Above him, Cyrus giggles and grabs his own knees, pulling his legs up.

"There baby, that better?"

Anton grunts an affirmative, diving immediately tongue-first to taste Cyrus at his core. His mouth explodes in a sweet musk, nose pressing hard against Cyrus's soft skin, tongue straining to reach deeper. Cyrus wiggles above him, clenching at the soft intrusion.

'Deeper. Need more. Taste more' Anton thinks to himself as he coils his tongue inside. He swirls it, using the thickness to spread

Cyrus's hole as much as he can, hands clutching desperately at the warm flesh of his hips.

Cyrus moans long and low above him, causing an echoed moan of pleasure to emanate from deep in Anton's throat. His breath exhales sharply against Cyrus's hole, wet from his spit, and he gasps as the temperature change registers.

"M-more please..." Cyrus asks, voice full of need.

Anton grunts again, nodding a little, before carefully bringing a hand down to tease the rim of his clenching hole. His eyes are closed as he's lost in the pleasure of making his Hyung feel good, a finger slipping carefully alongside his tongue.

He pulls his tongue out, remorsefully, replacing it with two fingers after salivating heavily on them in his own mouth, moaning again at the taste of Cyrus all over them.

"Mmm taste good" he whispers, sliding his fingers inside carefully. He pauses, wiggling the tips back and forth minutely for a moment, watching as Cyrus's face pinches together. He curls his hand, pulling them out, before thrusting forward hard.

Cyrus's face contorts, cheeks pink and flushed, as his hands fly out to clutch the bed.

"P-please Tony... Please"

"More?"

"More! Please please more" Cyrus begs, voice cracking.

Anton thrusts his fingers harshly inside, hips mirroring the movement against Cyrus's thigh as he clutched it to his belly. Cyrus keens loudly, head thrown against the pillows, hand reaching to grasp Anton's arm, when he adds a third finger.

"Y-yes! Yes, more."

    "C-can't... Need to... Want, ugh. Want." Anton's fried brain tries to put to words what he needs, praying Cyrus gets it.

He does. He nods frantically, hand tugging on Anton's arm, trying to pull his body closer. Anton leans in, Cyrus drops his legs to wrap around his hips and pulls him down for a kiss. Their tongues dance, flicking against each other, bouncing against each other's cheeks. They taste each other languidly, bodies writing softly against each other, sparking heat in every cell. Anton carefully pulls back, presses the tip of his cock against Cyrus's spit-slicked hole and presses gently before pulling back.

    He bounces, teasing the hole with just his tip, several times, right up until Cyrus's hand yanks at his scalp sharply.

"Tony,pleeeease"

    Anton's chuckle is soft, endearing more than taunting, because he gets it. He feels like it's not enough, not going to be enough, until he has given himself completely.

    'And taken Cyrus completely' he thinks, as he looks down at his lover, his boyfriend.

    "Mine...?" He asks, nosing at Cyrus's neck as he thrusts his fingers once more, flicking the tips back and forth when he's deep inside again.

Cyrus whines, nodding. "Yes baby. Yours. All yours."

    Anton pulls his fingers out, replacing them with his cock, and pushes in slowly. He nips at Cyrus's ear, licks his neck, cradles his head in one hand, as he slides further and further inside. "Mine" He whispers, over and over.

When Cyrus feels Anton fully seated inside him, he squeezes his legs and wraps both arms around Anton's neck. "And mine. Just us Tony"

"Just us" Anton whispers back as he slide their lips smoothly together again. They both rock their hips, slow movements when Anton pulls back, but hard as they punch inside again. Cyrus's body is rocked upwards each time, but his legs keep him locked to Anton.

Breathless, Anton pants above Cyrus, sweat slipping down his brow to pool at his Hyung's collarbone. "Pretty" he whispers, watching it slide further, to the bed. "So, so pretty"

Cyrus roams his hands, alternately clutching and sliding everywhere on Anton's skin he can. He wants him to know what touch is again, wants him to feel as loved and handled as he does.

"Gonna love you baby... Gonna love you s'long as I can okay?"

"And I you"

"Ahh.. ahh there Anton please there... please..."

Anton immediately focuses on the angle Cyrus is crying out from, moaning as he feels his body clench tightly around his cock. "Hnng?"

"Cl-close yeah... close..."

"Cum for me... Wanna... Wanna feel you around me"

"O....okay" Cyrus whines, hips flicking at Anton's pace as he nears his climax. His breathing pauses, then he gasps, then pauses again, breath held as he feels the familiar clenching and burning inside him.

"Y-ye-ye...yessss.... yes Tony m'close..."

"M-me too... can't... gonna" Anton gasps, belly heaving in ripples as he cums inside Cyrus's searing hot core, moaning loudly when he feels Cyrus clench around him soon after. "Shit... Holy shit"

Cyrus's voice is hoarse, crackling as he moans low in his register, vibrating against Anton's chest. Anton leans down and presses a kiss to his lips carefully, grinning wide.

"I love you. I love you so much"

"And I, you. My lover, my boyfriend, my sweet oak tree."

Cyrus pulls Anton close, keeping their bodies flush as they hold eachother.Eventheirtoescurlagainsteachother.Antoncarefully pulls out, pressing whomever's boxers are closest against Cyrus's ass to keep the sheets as clean as possible, wiping him gently.

And then, they curl against each other, with Anton wrapping his big oak arms around Cyrus's smaller frame, drifting off to sleep.

Cyrus wakes first, considerably earlier than he's accustomed to. He stretches slowly, fighting the very great urge to wiggle against his very warm Anton shaped human blanket. He deserves a medal for it, honestly. Especially when that unyielding shape starts to shift of its own accord. He holds his breath, slowly sliding out and down the edge of the bed, replacing his body with the warm blankets, nicely rolled up.

He leans back, plopping quietly onto his butt and winces, hissing immediately.

'Ah, shit, forgot about that' he thinks, gingerly leaning up onto his hands and knees. He pads quietly to the door, the soft scent of 'old' permeating his nose as he passes all of Anton's childhood things. He grins, wondering briefly what it smelled like before.

Reaching above his head, he slowly tugs on the handle, wincing and glancing backwards when it clanks slightly in the mechanism. Anton hasn't even breathed.

'Phew'

Crawling out of the room, he leans up on his knees to quietly bring the door to a dimmed click shut before sighing in relief.

And hears a dramatic crunch behind him.

He slowly turns and meets the gaze of none other than Javier Phillips, who stood leaning against the wall with a bag of chips, crunching another one even more dramatically than the last.

"So, crawl here often?" the elder grins, lips pursed cheekily.

"Oh, you know" Cyrus whispers with feigned nonchalance to match, "Been around once or... once..."

He awkwardly rises to his feet and shuffles down the hall towards the kitchen. He's stopped by Javier's arm, holding out the bag of chips.

"Ah, I wouldn't... Not unless you want to spend the next 45 minutes with the Aunties, and then getting roped into being a mule for them between the kitchen and the patio..."

Cyrus freezes, hesitating as he looks down at his bare feet and thin sleeping clothes. He glances back at the closed door and grimaces, shoulders slumping.

"So, that's why you're creeping about the hallway with your chips?"

"My friend, I was hardly creeping. I was minding my own business, eating my chips in my family home's hallway in peace." He grins and gestures the bag towards Cyrus.

"And you, weird little cat man, just crawled out of my cousins bedroom on your hands and knees. If anyone is creeping here, it's definitely not me." He crunches down on another chip, crumbs dusting the air in a tiny cloud.

Cyrus narrows his eyes at Javier and huffs.

"So, not-the-creeper, what do you propose we do? We can't sit here in the hallway eating chips all day, and Anton is still asleep."

Javier brings a finger up to his lips and smirks, jerking his head towards the bathroom door right across Anton's room. They both enter, one sitting on the edge of the tub and the other on the closed toilet lid.

"Soooo....?" Cyrus asks softly.

"So, how was your night?" Javier waggles his eyebrows suggestively, crunching on another chip much softer than he had been. Cyrus was grateful, because he'd started to wonder if the man was trying to break a record for loudest chip crunch.

"It was... a night... Did you really drag me into this bathroom to get the details of my night with your cousin?"

"Well, no, but, I don't exactly have any idea as to what you like other than Tony so..."

Cyrus stares blank-faced at Javier's upturned grin as he speaks and blinks at him. "I like music, I play piano and guitar mostly, I write lyrics on occasion, and my two best friends are romantically ambiguous extremely gay dancers. Your turn.”

Javier matches his bored tone and fires back immediately, “I like fishing, gaming, cooking and eating even though I’m sensitive to more foods than I can count... And I’d love to get the numbers of your romantically ambiguous extremely gay friends.”

He finishes with a wink that sends Cyrus into a hushed fit of laughter. Javier’s laugh is a loud bark at first until Cyrus lunges forward and claps his hands over his mouth.

“Shhhhh shh what is wrong with you how does a human make that loud of a sound are you kidding me?”

“Sorry! Sorry.”

“... I also like cooking” Cyrus says after they come down from their giggles.

“Sweet. Maybe we can set something up sometime? Cook together? You know, when we aren’t likely to be mauled in the kitchen by the auntie army?”

They chatter quietly back and forth for a little while. Mostly about favourite kitchen utensils, a little about Cyrus’s fingers being rough from guitar and a dash of Javier’s favourite spots for ocean fishing.

Cyrus hums in acknowledgement, holding a hand out for another chip.

They’re startled by a loud knock, chips falling to the ground before being hastily (And noisily) picked back up.

“Occupado!” Javier yells out as Cyrus stifles a giggle.

They hear a gravelly grunt from the other side before Cyrus
flies over and nearly rips the handle off the door. Anton blinks,
confusedly, seeing Cyrus when he knows he just heard a different
voice.

"Wha-" he starts, hushed quickly by a hand covering his mouth and
another yanking him into the bathroom and shutting the door.

"Cuz?" Anton mumbles, blinking at Javier on the toilet.

"Hey Tony" the elder replies nonchalantly. He lifts the bag in the
air and asks, "Chip?"

Anton swallows and turns his neck to look at Cyrus, face
etched with confusion. Cyrus smiles and brings him to the tub's
edge with him, hands softly pressed against his hips. He shivers
as he feels like a dozen little fingers dance all over him.

"Javier here may have lured me in here with chips and the
promise of eternal salvation of my soul... From The Aunties."

"Ahhh right. Auntie Mere is here, isn't she?"

Javier hums, nodding fervently.

"Thought so." Anton pulls Cyrus into a soft kiss, all lips and
love, before elaborating in a hushed tone. "Auntie Mere is our 2nd
cousin or something, technically, but she's the eldest of like, 8?"

"Seven" Javier corrects, head tipped back to keep the chip from
falling out. "But she counts that demon dog of hers as the 8th"

Anton shudders. "Elvis. She named him Elvis, after her
favourite singer, but she should have named him Demon. Or
Hellspawn. He likes no one, except Aunt Mere. But of course he
also only misbehaves when she's not around."

"He's a smart dog, really" Javier mumbles, "But by god he's a menace."

"What, is he a Mastiff or something?"

"Worse" Javier says.

"He's a Maltese" Anton finishes for him, their nose crinkling in tandem.

Cyrus just blinks at them, disbelieving. "A Maltese... Anton your shoes are bigger than a fucking Maltese..."

"Yeah, well... my shoes... don't have teeth. Or claws. Or a dick that has to mark every single thing it finds as its own terri...tor....y..." Anton trails off, blinking back at Cyrus, who has leveled a look at him.

"Really? Marking territory mm? That's what you're complaining about?"

Anton starts to argue, but Javier holds up a hand. "Little brother, just let him find out. There's no way he'll understand until then."

"Okay, so demon dog, eldest of many kids, is that all I need to know about Auntie Mere?"

The boys look at each other just as there's a resounding crash in the kitchen. Cyrus watches as the two Phillipss stand at attention, chips dropped, eyes wide. Before he can hear anything at all, they've bolted out of the bathroom and into the main living space.

"Ah, finally, some USEFUL people around here! Javi darling, do Auntie a favour and go find my little sunshower, yeah? It's about time for his medication. Tony dear, come give Auntie a hand."

Cyrus is all but ignored, for which he's unsure if he should be grateful or not, so he hovers off to the side out of the way. He jumps when he hears a feral growling from the other end of the hallway followed by a panicked scream. Looking at Anton, who is busy grabbing things Auntie Mere is too short to reach, he sees the man's eyes wide but no other reaction. The woman just smiles and says, "Ah, Javi always was little Elvis' favourite. I love hearing them get along so well."

Cyrus mouths at Anton, face concerned, "So well?"

Anton only shrugs and pinches his lips together in a grimace.

"Well? Don't just stand there young man, shoo shoo! Go sit, let Auntie get you something to eat, yeah? You're so little. Don't worry, we'll fatten you right up won't we Tony? Can't bear your children around on hips like that, can you?"

Cyrus frowns heavily, feeling his body sitting on the stool at the counter but not really registering it as he replays what she just said.

'Bear... children? I'm... that's not even... She knows I'm a man, she just called me a young man, so why-'

Anton, once again ever helpful, just shrugs and shakes his head as if to say "Don't ask". Cyrus decides to trust him this time. His family, his expertise. So he folds his hands on the counter and waits for... something... anything, to make himself feel useful.

That thing comes sooner rather than later.

Elvis, closely followed by a sliding Javier, comes bolting into the kitchen, darting under Anton's feet (Causing him to drop what he was holding, which thankfully was just a large metal mixing bowl) and skidding to a stop at the back door.

"Javi, you weren't supposed to chase him like that, he's getting old. He can't keep up with you kids anymore you know?"

"Yes Auntie, sorry Auntie." Javier bows a quick apology and tries to catch Elvis, but the tiny little cotton fluff dashes through his legs and skids into the rug on the other side, looking up at Cyrus.

He opens his mouth to bark, Cyrus beats him to it with a soft 'grr', wrinkled brow and squinty eyes included... And then he's trotting happily right over to Cyrus's feet, plopping into a crooked 'sit' position, patiently waiting for Cyrus to pick him up.

Javier looks at Elvis, then at Cyrus, then at Anton who looks equally flabbergasted, and they both look back to Cyrus again.

"How the fu-"

"Javier PHILLIPS. DON'T YOU DARE SAY THAT WORD WHERE MY DEWDROP CAN HEAR IT."

Javier jerks upright instantly and bows another apology, smiling sheepishly. "Yes Auntie, really sorry Auntie, I nearly forgot the cute little candy puff was even here, look how cute and good he is"

Auntie Mere's face softens like a switch has flipped, and suddenly Cyrus gets it. She is insane. She is certifiably, definitely 100% insane. Okay cool. He's trapped in a kitchen with a crazy lady and her alleged demon dog.

The demon dog that wants him to pick it up.

"Yes, my little raindrop is the perfect baby isn't he? It's too bad he can't have pups, he'd be such a good stud wouldn't you baby?" Auntie Mere has reached down to scrunch the dog's face in her hands, laughing as he licks at her.

She turns back to the kitchen and immediately moves around like she owns the place. Cyrus notices, though, how she gracefully side-steps and pulls in her elbows, to avoid touching Anton. She's innately aware of where his limbs are, and avoids them entirely.

He loves moments like this, where he can just observe. You see so many things you don't normally get to, when you're busy living the moment first-hand.

Like how Javier's shoulders are tense around the little dog, jerking back when he playfully nips at him, which just causes him to do it again thinking it's a game.

Or how Anton's still flinching himself when he feels Auntie Mere's clothes flutter against him, or how his hands shake a bit when he passes a bowl of ingredients towards her.

But he also sees how Javier's lips press together when he tries to hold his hand still, determined to get this dog to like him.

And how Anton's brows furrow when he pushes his hand a little closer to Auntie Mirae's, going so far as to graze their elbows once or twice.

"Little things" He muses aloud. "It's the little things."

"What'd you say sweetheart?" Auntie Mere asks, not bothering to turn around as she chops more vegetables.

"Life... It's got so many big things that steal our attention, but it's the little things... those are the ones that matter the most."

She turns to look at him, and winks with a wide grin, before jerking her head at Anton. "Why don't you take a big thing off my hands then, huh? The little one too. Maybe I'll find some wisdom in this sauce"

Cyrus smiles and nods back at her. "Yes Auntie, I'd love to." He tugs at Anton's elbow, pulling him out of the kitchen, stopping to scoop Elvis up on the way. Javier huffs out a protest, but stares when he realizes Elvis isn't fighting Cyrus at all. Looks content, in fact.

"How the-" He glances at Auntie Mere and clamps his mouth shut. The trio trudge into the living room and sit on the couch, the two Phillips' on either side of Cyrus, who perches Elvis in his lap. Within minutes, he has the pup doing tricks.

Colt, Josh, Jamie and Tyler eventually wander in to find Javier kneeling on the ground, watching Cyrus command the dog to twirl in a little dance with awe, and Anton draped over one of Cyrus's arms.

Jamie and Tyler drape their limbs across each other and the couch, Tyler sloping a long arm around Cyrus to lean on his free side. Josh and Colt squeeze into a chair nearby, arms around each other.

"Looks like you four got real comfortable real fast" Cyrus chuckles as he watches the others, booping Elvis' nose when he jumps up again.

Tyler's boxy grin is on full display as his rich voice laughs. "Oh you have no idea little bro. Speaking of comfort, what about you, cousin?" Tyler reaches a long finger to poke Anton's cheek softly.

He gasps when Anton turns and bites that finger with a grin. "Mm. Real comfy. Realllll comfyyy" He squeezes at Cyrus, reaching up to kiss the elder's cheek loudly.

Cyrus blushes, ignoring him, continuing to busy himself with the little white dog. That is, until Javier snatches him away and runs outside with him. He calls back, "Hah! He's mine now!!"

The back door lets in a cloud of chattering voices that has Anton tensing briefly. Cyrus squeezes a hand on his knee and whispers, "Okay?"

Nodding, Anton whispers back, "Gonna tell them. Gonna try and..."

"Hey, hey, you don't have to rush okay? This is a lot, you've done a lot already this week. Hell just in the last day. There's no rush, you know?"

"No, I know. I know there isn't really, but... There also kind of is? Some of these Uncles aren't getting younger. And... And most of them I have never hugged. I want that... I want to know that I loved them to the best of my ability."

Cyrus smiles fondly. "Baby you are. Even loving them as you do right now, without touch, you are loving them to the best of your ability. They know that, we know that. Right guys?" He turns to the others who have been listening intently.

Colt pipes up, "I just met you and I already know you love probably harder than anyone I've ever met. Sorry babe" he finishes, looking apologetically at Tyler.

Tyler shakes his head, "No you're right. I love you with all my heart Coltie but if you even hinted at me not touching you, even out of love, I think I wouldn't be able to do it. You two... You both did it out of love, and that's... that's big. Big love."

"I agree" Josh says, reaching over to hold Cyrus's hand in his own as the latter has started to tear up. "Anton stopped touching because he thought he hurt the people he loved when he did so. Even when that meant he couldn't be touched either."

"And Cyrus... He saw someone hurting, and before even understanding the how or why he figured out the what. What he had to do, what he had to not do. I'm sure it was hard… for both of you."

Auntie Mere's voice interrupts as she strides in, placing a tray full of sweet little pickled vegetable sandwiches on the table.

"Young people tend to think of love as one-sided. A thing you have, or don't have. A thing you do, or don't do. A thing you see, or don't see." She tuts, handing out a sandwich on a napkin to each of them.

"Love is none of those, and love is all of those. Love is felt, and untouched. Seen, and invisible. Heard, and silent. It is everything that is, and everything that isn't. You know?"

She smiles fondly and strides back out again, calling for Javier and Elvis.

The silence is broken when Jamie pipes up, "Did she make literally any sense?"

They laugh, because they know she made about as much sense as she didn't. They didn't understand her words, but they understood her meaning, and that's what mattered.

Anton inhales, standing up, shoulders squaring.

"Okay. Okay I'm going to do it. First, I'm gonna find my mom and I'm gonna hug her. Then, I'm going to find Uncle Emmit and I'm going to shake his hand. And then I'm gonna hug every single cousin."

"Yeah!! You hug 'em Tony!" the group erupts in cheers, rooting for their (big) little tree.

"Yes!Yeah.I'mgonnadoit.I'mgonna…Gonnahug'emSO HARD." His face scrunches immediately as his brain catches up.

"Er, no, not hard. Soft? No. Firm. Yeah, firm. I'm gonna hug 'em
SO FIRM." His fist punches the air in front of him, and Cyrus can't
help but giggle.

He wraps Anton in a hug from behind, inhaling the scent of his
boyfriend. "I believe in you, Tony. Whatever you're gonna do, I'm
right here with you, okay?"

"No more bubbles."

"No more bubbles then."

"Just a big oak tree."

A snort, then "My big sweet oak tree."

Anton melts backwards into the embrace with a deeply dimpled
grin on his face. "Yours."

☞ ☜

And so, the strangest Phillips family reunion in at least two
decades went off with every hitch you could imagine.

Javier chased Elvis around the yard, desperately screaming
"LOVE ME YOU LITTLE DEMON", much to the pup's delight. The
duo wreaked havoc, though, when Elvis darted under the table
where lunch was being piled, and Javier didn't stop fast enough.

If Elvis got ahold of some strawberries before running to Auntie
Mere looking like he slaughtered an animal, and if she then
screamed bloody murder and nearly caused Uncle Emmit to have
a heart attack... Well, who could blame them.

And if Julia cried no less than 14 different times, and had to be
pushed away from the kiddie pool for fear of "over-watering the

garden", only to find herself wrapped in Anton's arms once more... So what? Even if it meant they both tumbled head first into the flowers?

Tyler and Jamie were glued so tightly together, that Jamie was repeatedly addressed as 'Colt'. Colt didn't mind correcting them, though it definitely caused confusion considering he and Josh were wrapped around each other nearly as often.

The foursome left early, excusing themselves as needing to "check on Colt's father"... But Cyrus got a text later on from Josh saying they had all piled up at his parents' place, because they were out of town.

Eventually, he and Anton grabbed Javier by the neck, hand over his mouth to sneak him as quietly as Javier could be snuck, out of the house, to join their friends.

As midnight approached, Auntie Mere and Julia were the last ones up, tidying the last of the preparation and checking on the crockery.

"You did good, Julia" Mere nudged the woman, smiling softly at her.

"Did I Meredith? I just... All these years... My baby... Because I..."

Meredith tuts and pinches Julia's ear. "None of that. You didn't know, and he didn't know. You both made decisions based on the moment, that neither of you had full information of."

"He said something once... I think he blames himself for Carlos leaving. I just... Which path is better? The truth, or the belief?"

"What is the difference when they both hurt?"

Julia sighs, head firmly in her hands. "The belief means he blames himself. Which hurts me to think about. But the truth..."

"The truth hurts you both all the same. The difference is, the belief holds the double edged sword of Hope. He will spend his life with this belief, hoping that if he changes himself, his father will return."

Mirae pinches her lips together tightly.

"But you and I both know there is no such hope. You and I both know you spent half that boy's life sending every picture you ever took of him to that man, sent journals filled with events of his life every step of the way. Where did that get you?"

Julia looks away, grief etched on her face.

"Carlos... Carlos is a good man, Mere."

"Tsch. Good my left foot. He left you. He left his baby, his first-born son. He walked away from this entire family, and for what? A two-faced snake that betrayed him just as fast. It's his fault he chose her and it's his fault he fell for the bottle."

"It's not yours, and it's not little Tony's. Even if he isn't nearly as little as I left him last."

The humour sparks a glow in Julia's eyes, as intended, and Meredith rubs her arms tightly.

"We told you before. You are the Phillips. You are one of us. You became one of us the day you showed up here in Carlos' place, holding that sweet little bundle. He chose his path, we chose ours. And now, you must choose your own."

Julia nods, face falling again. "He's gonna be so heartbroken..."

Meredith nods back, humming thoughtfully. "But his heart will break around his father, instead of himself. Better that than for him to continue to doubt himself, or his worthiness of love, no?"

Elvis trots over, a discovered piece of pork in his mouth, tail wagging... And the ladies have to laugh. It's nearly twice the size of his head, but he is proudly attacking it with fervor.

"Ahh this is a good omen, I think. See Julia? Bounty is coming. Today was one step towards a blessed future, just you watch."

3 years later

"KELSEY-AHHHHH COME HERE RIGHT THIS INSTANT"
Cyrus yells after the girl, whose bare feet pound on the wood beneath them. Her squeals are only matched by the deep growling that follows her through the house.

"Hey! Anton you know she's supposed to be taking a nap."
Cyrus opines, arms crossed over his chest.

Anton looks up, face flushed, and grins. "I-She is! I'm just... tiring her out, honest!"

"Mhm. Well, if Papa tires himself out now" Cyrus leans down to pick up their daughter before whispering back at him with a grin "Then Papa won't have any energy left for playtime later, now will he?"

Cyrus's fingers tickle the toddler before the two disappear into the nursery.

When Cyrus returns a few minutes later, he's swallowed by thick arms around his waist.

"Papa always has energy for Dada, don't you worry about that." He growls, kissing Cyrus's neck softly.

The elder shivers, arms clutching his partner tightly. "I'm proud of you, Tony. You know that?"

Anton grunts and tucks his chin over Cyrus's shoulder. "Me too, I think. It's been... A lot, hasn't it?"

"Mm. Graduation, confronting your past, now Kelsey..."

"We really did all that, didn't we?"

"We sure did, love. Even got yourself a job where you shake hands every day!"

Anton groans and buries his nose in Cyrus's neck. "Ugh, please don't remind me. I kind of miss the days when I could just pretend I didn't need touch sometimes. At least at work."

Cyrus spins in his arms and stands on his toes to kiss the dimple that shows itself. "Well I don't. I like seeing you bloom like this, just like that little tree I gave you."

"Ah, right. My tiny orange tree."

"You mean me, right?"

They giggle in each other's embrace, quietly as to not wake the babe, relishing in the warmth that has persisted for the last few years.

And looking forward to the warmth of many more to come.